I0733777

JULIE BROWN

# Chained to a Dream
Truth=Freedom, Book 1
Julie Brown

ISBN: 978-1-959788-12-6

There is always freedom in truth.

"Let me be clear, the Anointed One has set us free-
not partially, but completely and wonderfully free! We
must always cherish this truth and stubbornly refuse to
go back into the bondage of our past." Galatians 5:1 (tPt)

Acknowledgements

To God, first and foremost- Thank you for giving me the love of writing. I truly have a dream job. Also, for bringing me through the corrections field safely. Although this is a fictional piece, the framework was based on experience and as anyone serving in a justice or mental health field of work knows, people are messy, and the world can be very dark. Despite my ability to see His hand in the process, He had a plan, and this book is the culmination of His guiding, compassionate love.

To my family- thank you for always reading my stories. I value your support.

To Cora, my crit partner- thank you for encouraging me to write better and stronger, for being honest in your critiques, and for "consoling" me when I need to edit, edit, edit.

To Paulette and Sherry- thank you for going on this journey with me. Your feedback was invaluable.

To Cordell- thank you for answering all of my crazy questions and agreeing to vouch for me if my questions got too much attention from… well, you know.

To Virginia and Charlie- thank you for brainstorming the "What ifs" and for your knowledge of the Spanish language. Any mistakes are mine.

1

She had to enter the darkness. *Just go. Just do it.*

Crouching, Selena Maldanado pulled her .38 out of its holster and slid it into the crack in the door. If anyone was in the darkness, they'd see her first. And wait. Wait until she was in the room, their eyes already adjusted to the blackness, watching as she blindly felt her way in.

Selena pushed her automatic further in the door. Rushing around the corner, she plastered her body against the wall. She was inside. The sweat rolled down her back, scurrying behind the heavy Kevlar vest. Her blood raced through its channels, only stopping long enough to slam into her heart and then back out to the extremities. The feeling echoed in her ears. Boom, boom, boom. If there was anyone in the room, they'd hear it, too. The taste of iron filled her mouth as adrenaline pumped through her body.

Now that her eyes had adapted, Selena could see she was alone in the square room. The walls were empty, void of any life-giving indications.

She removed her flashlight from one of the pockets on her belt and shone it around the room. The light pierced the darkness and lit up the room sufficiently. She scanned the baseboards for the package she had been told was somewhere in the building. Nothing.

Two closed doors were across from her. Standard doors could lead to anywhere. The hinges were on the left so the doors swung into whatever lay behind them. Ay, ay, ay. Which one to choose? Selena tried to remember what the building looked like from the outside. Long and wide. Both doors could lead into other areas or another room this size. But which one first?

Selena skittered diagonally across the room and wiped the sweat from her hands.

"On three," she whispered at the door on the left. If she didn't open it on three, she might never open it.

"One, two…" Selena turned the knob and allowed the weight of the door to swing inward.

Dust motes hung in the air as her illuminating torch danced around the room. An old, upright piano sat snug to the wall, removing any possible hiding place. Selena searched the floor. No footprints in the dust, no one had entered here in a while. The package wasn't in this room either.

Selena moved silently back out of the room. She lowered the beam of the flashlight to the floor and gave a quick look to make sure no one had snuck in while she was investigating the room behind the first door.

Hopefully, the next door would lead to

something useful.

Turning off the flashlight, she reached out. The handle was cold as if what lay beyond was colder. Selena heard the click as the door released from the frame.

Selena knelt and reached out a hand to touch the floor in front of her. Cool concrete met her fingertips unlike the wooden floor she was currently on. Damp air pushed against her face. Switching on her flashlight again, she could see a wall in front of her, more concrete. To the left, wooden stairs opened above a dark cavity. A face floated in front of her.

Selena stood and raised her gun, startled. On seeing the long, midnight black hair with wide dark eyes, she realized she was looking in a small oblong mirror. She watched her image lower the gun. Fumbling to find the light switch, she dropped the flashlight and heard it thump its way down into the abyss.

Por Favor! Why would anyone hang a mirror at the top of basement stairs? And where was the light switch? If the lights in the rest of the building didn't work, these wouldn't either, but it was worth a shot.

Selena swished her hand out in front of her, waiting to feel the chain or pull cord whisper across her outstretched palm. If something grabbed her from the darkness, she was history.

Pulling the rope, she heard the click. Nothing. No lights here either.

Selena stepped forward onto the concrete. If she shut the door, claustrophobia might get the best of her, like being sealed into whatever lay beyond permanently.

She listened for movement below. Selena scuffed her foot along the concrete edge to the drop of the first step.

The railing was wooden with splintery gouges down the 2x4s. Selena braced one hip up against the concrete wall and avoided putting any weight on the railing. Sliding down the wall, Selena kept her .38 leveled at the open darkness to her left. Nothing stirred. Musty odors assaulted her nose.

Reaching the bottom without incident, Selena pushed her toe around, searching for the flashlight. Her heavy leather boots clunked into it, and she bent to retrieve it.

Basta! Stop it! She'd watched too many scary movies and now every piece of darkness threatened to jump out at her.

Selena crisscrossed her wrists like she'd been taught, elbows bent slightly, gun resting over flashlight. With a click, shadows appeared against the rough cement walls. A very roughhewn basement from the looks of it. The dirt floor was tracked up like many people, and things, had passed through recently. Selena shone the light under the steps. Nothing. The green duffle bag marked Bank of Tanahey County wasn't there.

Old wooden shelves filled the opposite wall with dusty canning jars lined up neatly. Faded writing etched on the labels identified the contents. More jars were stacked behind cobwebs in the corner.

She was going to have to go farther into the cavernous cellar.

A short corridor led into a windowless room

crowded with furniture, old appliances, and junk. Selena could only partially see the area due to a large bookcase and off-colored cooler blocking her view. Selena bounced the light off the ceiling; no one could hide there; it was just exposed wooden beams.

Selena followed the tracks around several stacks of magazines and an old washer. She tensed as she heard the rustling of little claws in the papers.

Remember, you're Selena Grace Maldanado, no fear allowed. The dampness under her arms and across her chest belied the thought.

The next corner brought her to the base and front side of the big bookcase. Solid wood, it held no books, but served well as a barrier to the rest of the room. She tried to push it with no luck. She lifted a corner and pulled it a few degrees to the left. Enough to squeeze between the bookcase and the rusted doorless freezer...and there it was.

Army green duffle with white lettering stenciled on its side. Selena pulled the zipper open and peeked at the contents. Oh, yeah. Marijuana stacked nicely like small bales of hay and multiple full pill bottles jostled against each other. The stench was unmistakable, and Selena squinted her eyes at the onslaught of potent fumes. Ay, ay, ay. Just carrying the bag might cause her to feel high.

Standing, Selena illuminated the other part of the room looking for an exit door. She could go back the way she came; she didn't need light for that. Or she could look for a closer exit. Her flashlight lit up the concrete walls and she could see another darkened hallway. Praying she wouldn't run into anything alive, Selena hefted the duffle bag over her shoulder and made her way to the opening. Steps leading up to a door were shored up with wooden planks. A cool breeze blew around the door frame and she could see bright sunlight peeking through wormholes. She'd be out in fresh air after three short steps.

An arm shot out of the darkness, wrapping itself around Selena's middle.

2

Trapping the gun at her side, the man pressed his arm hard just under her ribcage. Both the gun and flashlight clattered to the floor and the duffle bag shifted. Towering over her, he jammed his forearm across her windpipe.

Selena struggled to breathe. Caught in the crook of his elbow, her eyes were level with an evil-looking tattoo.

The man shifted behind her.

Selena gulped in air stained with a strange mixture of sweat and cologne. Where did she know that smell from?

She went limp, allowing her whole body to sag in his arms. Dropping her chin under his arm, Selena waited, flat footed, but ready. As the man adjusted her weight in his arms, Selena moved, hands searching for his face.

Those are his ears, her palms told her. Slide your thumbs forward along the jaw line. She quickly traced his scruffy mandible bones until she found the soft spot under his chin. In one swift movement, Selena dug her thumbs into the skin as if to pull the bones straight out of his head. A good rake with her boot across his shin followed by a heavy stomp, and she was free of the stranglehold.

Off balance, both tumbled to the dirt floor scrambling for the gun.

Selena reached the gun first and crouching on one knee, she pointed it at the man. He pushed up into a seated position against the wall. Selena stood and inched toward him, flipping on the red laser and training it on his chest.

The man jumped up. "Okay, game's over, Maldanado."

"You didn't tell me part of the exercise was being attacked, Special Agent." She traced the FBI badge on his belt with the laser and danced the red dot across his taut t-shirt.

"This is training." Special Agent Jeremy Holtz snorted. "If I told you everything that would happen, it wouldn't be training now, would it?"

"Dude, if you ever do that to me again…" Selena refused to turn off the laser. It made such an impact.

"You're going to what?" The special agent stepped toward her.

Click. Selena racked the slide, another effective sound if the gun was loaded. She picked up the duffle bag and threw it at his feet. "Mission accomplished."

Selena ran up the steps and banged on the double doors. Mid-afternoon sky greeted her as she burst through the other trainees gaping at her and stripped off the bullet-proof vest. Between the adrenaline and her temper, her t-shirt was soaked. The guys ogled her curvy frame until she glared at them. Men are morons. How dare he grab her. It was supposed to be a simple find-the-bag exercise and learn how to maneuver flashlight and gun effectively. She'd allowed the adrenaline to get the best of her judgment. When Special Agent Holtz reached out of the darkness, she thought the Boogeyman himself had joined her in the cellar. Good thing, there weren't any cameras; she probably looked like a trapped wild animal. She'd lost her cool head. She knew exactly what cops who beat speeders at the end of a chase felt like. She'd lost control.

Ron DeNickey, her supervisor and lead investigator at the prison, approached with his hands waving a white shirt. "I surrender, I surrender."

Shut up. He acted like she was going to beat him up. She *had* pointed a gun, empty though it had been, on a FBI agent and *had* come away with the upper hand. The point of the lesson, though, was to keep a level head during any encounter and not let adrenaline rule. She'd failed that test. All she had wanted to do was pull the trigger. With a big impact. Not a good sign.

Selena waited while the scenario was reset, and the duffle bag replaced in the dirty cellar junkyard. A new victim, a guy from a local police department this time, was sent through. The only female at the law enforcement training conference, she should have expected the training officer would give her the exercise a little differently. She had ridden down with DeNickey for the weekend conference, at his suggestion, and although most of it had been lectures, this was the part she lived for.

The rush of emotions and ready-to-fight-attitude was who she was. She couldn't imagine being a part of any other career field. Bad guys, guns, a steady flow of crisis; it's what kept her blood pumping. Why she got out of bed in the morning.

She wasn't truly part of this group, though. Neither was DeNickey. The men talking with each other around her were from police departments in the area; she was law enforcement, too, inside a men's correctional facility, not on the street. They regarded her as one of them, most times, because a woman working in a men's prison had to be tough, and she'd proven herself numerous times. Being promoted to the investigative unit had been a dream and despite DeNickey's questionable motives, Selena was holding her own.

The police officer who went through the training activity after her was let out through the same doors. Dripping sweat, he peeled out of the jacket and holstered his firearm. Special Agent Holtz followed him out, equally drenched from the unventilated cellar.

Catching her eye, Special Agent Holtz stalked over to her side.

"Okay, gentlemen . . . and ladies, you all did a great job through Round 1. Now we begin the second half. How many of you think you know where we are?" Special Agent Holtz scanned the group. Several hands shot up. "Okay, then. Any good officer knows where they are at any given moment. You were brought here in state vehicles, but here's the second half. Each of you have been given a number. Find the person who has your matching number. This is your partner. In twos, I want you to return to the classroom. Last two back buy dinner. Any questions?"

People raised their numbers to match up with their partner. The group shifted to make sets of twos. Selena turned her card up, looking for her comrade. Sure, hope it's not DeNickey.

Selena saw Special Agent Holtz turn his card to her. Three, her match. Ugh.

"What's up with that?" Selena put her hands on her hips.

"Don't want to be paired up with the trainer, the man who holds all the answers?" Special Agent Holtz smiled at her. An irritating Cheshire-Cat smile.

"It just means a girl will have to do all the work for you. You may have all the answers, but I'm not asking. I don't need a partner." Selena resisted the urge to kick dirt on his boots.

'Too bad, you've got one anyway." Special Agent Holtz looked over the group. "Everyone ready? One hint, it's on the other side of the trees."

Groans sounded across the class.

"The building is surrounded by trees." One yelled out.

"Sure is. Find your way home, boys. And girls." Special Agent Holtz spun on his heel and paced off to the supply box. Picking up his .45, he loaded it and holstered the firearm. "In case, the Boogeyman shows up."

"Ha, ha." Selena moved away from the building and listened to the sounds around her. Groups of men huddled, discussing their plan of action. Soon they split up and went in their own directions. Selena walked to a nearby tree and jumped up, catching a lower branch. Pulling with her stomach muscles, she flipped her feet up and brought her body in line with the tree. If she could climb a little higher, she could see more, see a little farther.

"What are you doing?" Special Agent Holtz' strong voice carried below her.

"Looking around." Selena smiled when she remembered a time when she and a friend were playing tag with four-wheelers in a corn maze. Gaining a better view by standing on the four-wheelers, they were able to look over the tall corn stalks. The tree provided the same boon.

"See anything? I mean anything I'm not already aware of?" Special Agent Holtz smirked.

Selena resisted the urge to shake down a hailstorm of walnuts. Jumping to a lower branch and onto the ground, she brushed off her camo pants and slung the backpack over her shoulder. Without a word, Selena walked behind a Morton building and headed east. Special Agent Holtz chuckled and followed her lead.

After several minutes of hiking through dense underbrush, Selena tangled in a wild rose bush. The thorns buried themselves in her cotton T-shirt and wound around her torso.

"Need help?" Special Agent Holtz breathed over her shoulder.

"Nope." Selena reached gingerly behind her and pulled a pair of gloves from a side pocket of her backpack. "Always prepared."

Selena pushed through the remaining thicket and stumbled onto an old deer trail. Deer were pretty predictable; their tracks either led to water, a bedding spot, or a food plot. Selena turned north on the trail, hoping to see large, open spaces, instead of the confining brush or a water source. Cleared areas usually meant roads which had to lead to civilization and the designated building.

The deer trail opened onto a larger path which crossed a paved road after several yards.

"Going to take the obvious?" Special Agent Holtz looked both ways down the roadway.

Selena hesitated. Studying his face, she debated her decision. He could be playing with her, or he could be just asking a question. He stood still, meeting her direct gaze. She wouldn't trust him. She might do the obvious, but she might not. Her choice.

Irritated, she angled to what she thought was north and followed the road, walking on the grassy side. Others had passed by judging from the boot marks in the mud.

~

Special Agent Jeremy Holtz grinned at Selena's obvious distrust of him. She'd better trust her own instincts and no one else's. Many a recruit had trusted a senior partner and not his own gut level feeling and ended up maimed, scarred, or dead. Not to say a person shouldn't trust their partner, but he always trained in his classes to trust their inner voice first.

He'd kind of laid one on her when he attacked her in the training exercise. She was doing well under pressure, in a dark room with a time limit and a gun in her hand. It had been interesting to see her response when he increased the stress limit and jumped her. She was not nearly as tall as he was, but long legs created an illusion of height. And the curls? On a Latina? Wow. When he decided to ratchet up the game and add his own twist, his first thought was to grab a handful of hair as she walked by and see how she responded. He might lose a hand in that mop. Walking behind her, he could see that her whole figure was . . . well, it was a nice view.

"So, Maldanado," Special Agent Holtz caught up to her, matching stride for stride, "Why are you in this class? You're not a police officer, you're not county or federal."

Selena scowled at him, obviously annoyed. "What difference does it make?"

"None, really. Except I'm your instructor at the moment, and I'm asking." the Special Agent snorted. She was down-right snotty.

Selena stopped and crossed her arms. Special Agent Holtz stopped, too. They were squaring off? She was really peeved with him.

"Fine. My boss, DeNickey, sent me. Know him?" Selena moved away from him and on down the road.

"Yeah, I know him. Someone forced you to attend my class? Ha." He baited her. It was fun to see smoke roll out of her ears.

"NO," Selena stopped again. "Look, let's have it out right now. You had no right to assault me in the training. Who do you think you are? What I should have done is...forget it." Selena blew out a breath, stomping back onto the path.

"Hey, you brought it. Finish it." Maybe he had overstepped, but now she thought she had the upper hand? "Get back here, now."

"Or what?" Selena spun to face him.

"Look," Special Agent Holtz spread his hands in

front of him, "I think we got started wrong." Walking up to where she had dug her heels in, he cautiously tapped her forehead. Selena stepped back out of his reach. "You came in so confident. So sure you knew what you were doing. If I didn't shake it up a bit, you'd never have the opportunity to learn what you'd do under surprise. I wanted to see how you'd respond to an unpredictable situation."

"Really. You're an opportunist, then?" Selena shifted her duffle bag.

The negotiator in him kept her talking. "No, I'm a trainer. I train you for different scenarios, different set-ups, reactions, methods. But you are pretty fun to rile up."

Selena scrutinized him.

"Now you aren't threatening to shoot me, knock my head off, or spit in my face, tell me again why you're in my class? And not because DeNickey made you. I doubt anyone could make you do what you don't want to do."

Selena huffed. "Nope. I didn't hear a 'sorry'."

"Won't either." Special Agent Holtz laughed. "Come on, we're not far now."

Walking down the road again, Selena said, "Well, if you know DeNickey, you know where I work."

"Yes, at the prison. But in the investigative department with him?"

"Yeah, I rolled in as an investigator after guard duty for a couple of years." Selena hitched up her pants.

"Fully loaded, you could weigh almost six hundred pounds." Special Agent Holtz stepped ahead of her.

"Excuse me?"

"Easy, chica, I was referring to your gear." Special Agent Holtz huffed out a breath. This little wildcat could double as a porcupine. Everything he said offended her. "Back to the job. Why did you take up this class? It's not as if you're patrol and need to know where you're at. Or plan to enter a dark building by yourself for any reason. I can see the hostage negotiation part of the class but not the rest. I know, you wanted to meet me." Why was he intent on pushing her buttons?

"Sorry, didn't know you existed."

"You do now." Special Agent Holtz walked backwards in front of her.

"Yes, and how lucky do I feel? Let me count the ways." Selena said, dryly. "I just wanted to know everything, okay? Whether or not it applies to my job now, it might somewhere down the road. Speaking of which…"

The end of the pavement opened into a parking lot filled with squad cars and newer company cars. Low-lying buildings tucked behind huge oak trees served as the FBI training ground and a tall flagpole hosted a flag bearing the government emblem flapping in the breeze.

"Welcome to my world." Special Agent Holtz decided he might miss the smart-mouthed, long-legged investigator walking in front of him when his portion of the classes concluded.

3

The classroom was full of men in uniforms, sheriff department, police, plainclothes detectives and their gear, tossed under chairs and around the wall perimeters. Selena squeezed in between two hulky officers and planted her bag by her feet. Despite all of the testosterone in the room, she could endure for a little longer. And DeNickey was on the other side of the room, no need for conversation at all.

"I'm looking for a girlfriend," Special Agent Holtz said, passing in front of Selena. Silence greeted his statement. Then, a few chuckled. His lazy smile brought grins around the classroom. She, however, rolled her eyes. Men would always be morons.

After rushing into a black hole, losing her flashlight, wrestling and pulling a gun on Special Agent Holtz, and traipsing through the woods with him as her partner, Selena didn't feel the need for a personal conversation. Look for a girlfriend on your own time.

"Yeah, I know. You're all tired. You've chased shadows in the basement and found your way home today. By the way, #8 team, you're buying tonight.

You were the last in." Holtz pointed to a couple of men by the door. "I hope you've picked up good tactical information that will serve you in your job." Special Agent Holtz paced in front of the group. "But I truly am looking for a girlfriend. An undercover one. If you know of anyone, you can get in touch with me at the bureau or training office. Maldanado, if you decide to stop hating me long enough to consider it, call me."

Several of the men near her sent appreciative glances.

She wanted to slap each and every one of them. And Special Agent Holtz twice.

"Go get the bad guys and stay safe." Special Agent Holtz scooted tight-fitting jeans back up on the desk.

Waiting for some of the men to dissipate, Selena stayed in her chair and caught Special Agent Holtz staring at her. Brazenly, she held his gaze. He didn't intimidate her. And she definitely wouldn't consider the girlfriend suggestion. Special Agent Holtz smirked at her. Ugh. He was annoying.

DeNickey was still seated, talking to a tall, silver-haired gentleman in brown garb, a local Sheriff's department officer. No hurry there. Looking at Special Agent Holtz again, Selena pictured him out in the field. Motorcycle leathers, stubbly shadow. Was he always arrogant? She had to admit, on him, arrogance looked self-assured. DeNickey was conceited, but sleazy with his winks, greasy hair, and rotund body. And Special Agent Holtz was in a way different physical category with his dark T-shirt stretching across a broad well-defined chest.

Selena glanced at his ring finger. Not even a shadow of a ring. Of course, it didn't mean anything. DeNickey reportedly had women in several correctional facility towns. Why men chose infidelity was beyond her.

Standing, Selena crossed to the snack table and picked through the leftover chip bags.

"I lost you on the girlfriend thing?" Special Agent Holtz stopped next to her.

"No. Just not interested." Popping the bag open, Selena munched on the chips. Looking down at his scuffed boots, she wondered why he was still standing there. Couldn't he get the hint? She . . . was . . . not . . . interested. He was more of an idiot than she thought. "What do you want from me?"

Special Agent Holtz smiled.

"Go away. I've taken your class, you've assaulted me, forced us to be partners. What do you want?" Selena wanted to stomp her foot in exasperation.

"Just to see you aggravated."

"Well, you got it."

"Yep. Wanna be my girlfriend?" He said over his shoulder as he walked away from her, pant cuffs whispering against the tiled floor, his arrogance mixing with a hint of cologne.

Selena watched him leave the room. Que tonto. What a fool. The whole trip was giving her a headache.

~

Later that evening, Selena pulled on her jeans and a black T-shirt. Fresh from a nap and a shower, she prepared for the night out with the boys, some of the others at the conference who were going to dinner. Unfortunately, DeNickey was joining them as well.

DeNickey knocked on her door.

"Just a second." She'd made a crucial error by riding down to the conference with him, now she was without a car or any independence.

Selena opened the door a crack and slid out. There was no way she'd let him into the room if there was a possibility he took it as an invitation to stay.

"Ready?" DeNickey gave her an approving once-over. "Yes, you are."

The man made her skin crawl.

The restaurant was in the heart of the city on a block where loud music spilled out onto the sidewalk, and people jumped from bar to bar, looking for entertainment of any form.

Selena crowded beside a familiar face and left DeNickey to find his own spot somewhere away from her. Joe wore a wedding ring and had been polite to her throughout the conference.

"Hi." Selena stuck out her hand.

"Hello. Hey, sorry about the harassment you're getting."

"Thanks. Seeing as I'm the only female in this group I kinda expected it." It was refreshing not to have to defend herself or keep up with the barbs and vocal jabs.

"Well, you seem to be doing alright, but it's not my favorite thing to watch."

"Thanks again." Selena looked around in time to see Special Agent Holtz walk through the door.

Darn it.

"Special Agent." Her colleague acknowledged the training officer.

"Bristol. Good to see you in class." Special Agent Holtz shook his hand. "Maldanado."

"Special Agent." Selena pasted a cool smile on her face. Boy, he certainly smelled good.

"How's it going?" Bristol asked him.

"I'm still hoping Maldanado will agree to go undercover as my girlfriend."

A deceptive flutter worked its way up her chest.

4

Bristol glanced at Selena.

"Not on your life." Selena shook her head.

"Why? I thought we worked pretty well together." Special Agent Holtz provoked her, nudging Officer Bristol with his elbow.

"Not unless I have a gun in my hand, cowboy." Selena motioned to the barkeep. "A menu?"

"I don't think they serve rabbit food here." Holtz nodded at her slight frame. "Can't eat much more than that."

"Really? Shows what you know. I can eat way more than you." Selena challenged, scanning the menu.

"No way. Tiny thing like you?" Holtz puffed out his chest. "I'm not thinking so."

"Ok, bring us both a plate of those little hamburger sliders. He's buying." Selena hooked a thumb at Holtz.

Special Agent Holtz muscled onto the other side of Bristol, closer to Selena.

"You're going to eat a whole plate?" Bristol asked her.

"Yeah, and faster than him." Selena pulled a

napkin out of its container and put it on her lap.

"Bring it." Holtz grinned, ignoring the napkins. Turning his back to the barkeep, Holtz scanned the room. DeNickey, Selena's boss, was on the other side of the room, eyeing the dance floor.

On short order, two plates were placed in front of Selena and Holtz, piled high with small greasy hamburgers. Steam rose off the fresh, dripping burgers.

Selena's mouth watered as she anticipated the juicy fare.

"Ready?" Holtz picked up a slider. "Let's go."

Selena took a bite and watched as Holtz shoved the entire thing in his mouth.

"Wow," Bristol whistled. "Pretty serious."

"Hope you choke." Selena took two more bites. The hamburger was full of flavor with a hint of bacon and seasoned perfectly. A final mouthful ended the first slider. Holtz continued to chew.

Four more down, and Selena began to sweat. She was halfway through the plate with three to go. He cannot win.

Despite her small bites and Holtz' mouthfuls, they were neck-and-neck.

Selena took a sip of water, washing the rest of the burger down.

"Come on, Maldanado. Let's do this." Holtz picked up his glass in one hand and the last slider on his plate with the other.

Selena gingerly picked up hers. Only one to go. She'd never eat another one of these again. Grease rumbled through her stomach.

Two large bites and Selena quickly finished her

burger. Smiling to the best of her ability, Selena tried to keep the bile from rising in her throat.

"Nice job. Now if you'll excuse me." Holtz moved towards the men's restroom.

"I think I'm going to puke." Selena said to Bristol, covering her mouth with her hand.

"Over there to the bathrooms, but if you'd rather do it outside, the exit door is just a little further." Bristol moved away from her.

Selena stumbled to the exit and sunk to her knees under the one light shining in the back. Feeling the nausea race up from her gut, she spewed grease onto the rocky ground, aware someone had joined her. Ack, gross.

'Maldanado? You okay?" Hands pulled her curly hair into a ponytail at the nape of her neck.

Spitting the remains from her mouth, Selena accepted the cool bottle of water handed to her. She rinsed her mouth out and sat back on her haunches, looking up at her comforter. Holtz. Great.

He smiled at her and released his hold on her hair.

Selena closed her eyes. Tough girl just puked in front of the FBI.

"Hey, Maldanado. Look at me."

"What?" Selena stood, her knees shaky.

"I puked, too." Holtz laughed,

He handed her a mint from the bar. "Guess neither of us can handle our burgers." He chuckled again.

"Not many at least. Let's not do that ever again." Selena conceded. She glanced at him. He didn't look the worse for wear. She, on the other hand, had dust on her knees, knots in her hair and she could feel mascara clumped in the corners of her eyes. What a mess. Selena joined him on the crates near the door.

"Since we've shared this lovely experience, do you think you could call me Jeremy now?"

"I guess. You can still call me Maldanado." At his raised eyebrows, she added, "Just kidding. My first name is Selena."

After a silent moment, Selena said, "Thanks for holding my hair. Nobody's done that in a while."

"You puke often? Sorry, not called for." Holtz pulled a strand into the palm of his hand. "I kinda liked it. Not the puking part, holding your hair."

Heat rising in her face, Selena unwound it from his grasp.

"Hey, do you think we could start over? Be a little more friendly?" Jeremy suggested.

"Sure." Selena hopped off the makeshift bench and re-entered the building.

~

"Next time I'm in town…" Jeremy sat on the crate for seconds after she'd left. He'd taken her challenge and tried to beat her, but the grease-sodden burgers had the same effect on him they had had on her. Almost missing the trash can in the men's restroom, he'd thrown up every bit.

Holding her hair back as she violently lost the contents of her stomach had been a natural thing to do. Unfortunately, once he had his fingers in her hair, he wasn't much use to her. He knew her curls would be soft, but he hadn't expected the weight of them. Or how they curled around his fingers.

She'd allowed him a small piece of

vulnerability, not the wild cat with her claws spiked out that he'd seen earlier today. It had been quickly disguised as indifference when she left him.

"Women." Jeremy muttered as he walked back in the door. They were sure a confusing lot.

"Ah, here you are." DeNickey staggered against him.

Jeremy recoiled. Why did he have to be involved with this disgusting man? From the moment he had connected with the prison investigator, he'd regretted the decision. Every encounter had dripped with verbal garbage, from his nasty comments about women to his filthy choice of words. Still, he'd made a choice, and there was no way to back out. He could only hope this job would be done soon.

5

Brandon Rollos lifted the old-fashioned receiver and dialed the ten-digit number. He flicked dust from his gray institutional pants.

"You are receiving a collect call from an inmate in the Oklahoma State penitentiary system." An automated voice spoke in his ear. "Inmate, please state your name and number."

Brandon said the required information. A call to Suzie Winters always made him feel more like a human being rather than a number. Suzie was like a sister to him, and he knew it was testing her emotionally to see him in prison.

"Do you accept the charges?" The robotic messenger asked the person on the receiving line.

"Yes." Suzie's voice came across strong and sure.

"Thank you. All calls made from the penitentiary are subject to monitoring. You may proceed." A click and the two human voices were free to speak knowing the parameters of the possible recording.

"Hey, how are you?" Brandon said with his back to the other inmates in the yard. The phones in the housing units were more accessible and less crackly but also easier to eavesdrop on. The bouncing basketballs and loud conversations behind him provided the wanted privacy.

"Better now you've called. I was starting to worry."

"You knew it was going to take time. You worry too much," Brandon told her.

"Hey, it's not every day your closest friend goes to prison."

"You know I'll be fine. All those Kung Fu movies I watched may come in handy though."

"You're not very funny."

"Suzie, I'll be fine." Good friends didn't come around often, and despite being separated by bars, he wanted the relationship to remain intact. Nothing about prison life was easy and being away from loved ones was the worst.

"Okay, I won't ask again. Maybe. Tell me how you are really?"

"Well, the guards are unfriendly, but my cellmate is okay. He's a lot younger. I think he's adapting. Maybe too well."

"Can I send you anything?"

"If you can, keep putting money on the books for me." It was a lot to ask, putting money on an inmate's canteen account. He'd owe her big time when he got out.

"Sure. Anything else?"

"I could use information on a guard or two. Just for leverage, should it ever come up." Brandon prayed whoever monitored these phone calls was napping. He was taking a huge gamble saying anything over the phone lines. "One is a guard called Pig Eyes, I think his last name is Michaels. The other is a Latina that works out of the Investigator's office. Name's Maldanado."

"What kind of info?"

"Anything you think is relevant."

~

Back at work after the conference was over, Selena anticipated the everyday grind of working with inmates. At the airlock, Selena opened her briefcase for the guard to peek in.

"Nothing but lunch, a lovely peanut butter sandwich."

"Ew." the guard zipped it shut. "Anytime you want something from the cafeteria, you let me know, Maldanado."

"Ew." She mimicked him. "Fast food maybe, but not the cafeteria."

Descending the stairs to her office, Selena entered to the smell of mold growing somewhere and a last determined whiff of air freshener she'd plugged into the wall. Locking her briefcase in the file cabinet, Selena looked at the growing stack of papers on her desk. Aye, yi, yi. Lately, there were more than the usual hot weather clashes between inmates, which always generated paperwork. A full moon or extreme weather, hot or cold, often brought out the ugliness in people.

Because the correctional facility held 2,000 men, and the majority of the staff were male, Selena navigated carefully through the testosterone-filled egos. Always aware of who was around, who she was walking with, who she spoke to, and who they spoke to. She smiled at the thought of so many Banty Roosters scratching their way across the fenced-in yard. Ruffling feathers or soothing them down were all part of the game.

"Morning." DeNickey entered her office and set his ever-present cup of coffee on her desk. "Lots of work today. The fight in the gym last night landed a bunch of them in the hole. Head there first."

As she took the files from him, his hand brushed hers. Did he do that on purpose? She shook her head. If he weren't her immediate supervisor, she would never go near this man.

Through two air locks and back into the fresh air, Selena took a shortcut through the prison yard to the locked down housing unit. Inmates assigned to lawn maintenance were digging out weeds by the sidewalk and she could see others working among the garden rows.

She sure didn't have a green thumb, everything in here would be as brown as the institutional walls.

Selena stiffened her back and walked resolutely to the "Hole" as many called it. Fifty yards in front of her sat a few inmates at a bench near one of the yard's basketball goals. Covered in baby powder, a trick some had learned to keep the sweat to a minimum, the men watched Selena approach them.

No one said anything until she was upon them. Knowing intimidation was a sign of strength, she kept her eyes locked on the biggest of the trio.

Speak first and talk to the pack leader.

"Hello." Selena stopped in front of them.

"Hey, Momma. How's the heat?" the big one asked. Selena ignored the slang. She could push it, requiring him to address her formally or she could pick her battles.

"Over a hundred degrees. Enjoy the sun, gentlemen." Selena moved on down the sidewalk. Hoping she looked confident, she felt a trickle of sweat run between her shoulder blades. It never ended well if the inmates spotted weakness. Anything soft was taken advantage of, often by inmates and guards alike.

Selena's father worried about her working in the prison and it had taken a while for her to tell him the whole title of her employer, Oklahoma State *Men's* Correctional Facility.

Although Selena didn't carry a gun, she had other leverage over the inmates, and her best defense was attitude. Carrying herself with as much bluff as she could, Selena led most of the men into believing she could hold her own in any situation. An occasional tongue lashing in Spanish didn't hurt the image, although her mouth got her in more trouble than out of trouble.

She walked the final few yards to the locked-down unit and entered, the cold AC starting a migraine behind her eyes. This was the loudest unit with cat calls and screeching coming from inside the cells.

6

"Wow. Smile and all," Sam Matthews, the housing unit supervisor, teased. Almost twice her age, he never failed to make her laugh and release the tension for a moment. Plus, he had an endless supply of diet soda always available.

"What? A girl can't smile?" Selena's grin increased, showing white, even teeth.

"Not like that. Not in here." Sam reached in a drawer and brought out a warm can for her. Leaning out the door, he called one of the officers, "Hey, Doug. Can you give the clerk some ice?"

"You are probably the only housing unit with ice."

"I bring it in a cooler from the admin building. Keeps the guards happy."

"What's it looking like today?" Selena pointed at the board where inmates' names were listed along with cell numbers.

"We've got thirty-five in segregation for the lovely fight you're here for. Forty who just came off the bus, so they'll sit with me for a bit. Forty-five are in protective custody and a solid fifty bozos for random violations."

"A full house, then."

"Yeah, I don't get it. They're already in prison, do something stupid to get sent to the Hole, and then they lose all their privileges except for the one hour a day we let them out in a cage. Beyond me."

A gray-clothed inmate handed two cups of ice to Sam through the narrow opening between the desk and the door.

"Thanks, Brandon."

Selena watched as the inmate delivered the ice. He didn't look at her or Sam but simply handed off the cups without a word.

"What? Why are you smiling at me?"

"You're just nice to everyone."

"No, I'm not. But he's a human being like we are. No reason for disrespect." Splitting the diet drink, Sam poured it into each of their cups. "If you're ever looking for an inmate clerk, he's a good guy. Brandon Rollos."

"I'll keep that in mind."

"What brings you down to the pit of hell?" Sam asked. "Me, I suppose."

"Your fighters for one." Selena pushed a lock of hair back. "I have to do some interviews, but I also wanted to tell you about this guy I met at the conference. Jeremy. He's FBI." She blushed.

"FBI? Wow, you're moving up. From little old me to FBI?" Sam frowned playfully at her.

"You know you'll always be number one in my book. However..." Selena felt her face flush.

"Your ears are red. Spill it, what happened?"

"Jeremy was one of the instructors at the conference, and he was incredibly irritating at first.

Then he was joking about looking for a girlfriend, and I thought he was a little arrogant. But it's a legit undercover job." Selena chipped a piece of Styrofoam off her cup with a fingernail. "I guess I looked perfect for the job."

"Perfect undercover…or perfect as a girlfriend?"

Selena looked up at Sam's tone. Was he jealous? Protective? Selena added "wary" to her growing definition of emotions on Sam's face. His blond crew cut and nearly white beard paled further under her scrutiny. Selena felt she could read him fairly well, but something in his voice unsettled her.

"Undercover." Indignant, Selena ignored Sam's raised eyebrows. "I didn't agree to anything even though DeNickey seemed to think it would be a good idea."

"Of course, he did."

Selena felt the heat in her face intensify.

"You know how I feel about DeNickey. I'm not saying it again."

"I'm not sure you should say it at all since he's my boss."

"Look, I know investigative work has been your goal since you took this job and I know that you're thinking career moves, but I'm not sure what these guys are thinking. DeNickey's a snake, and the only good thing about him is his title. I don't know this FBI character but if he's in cahoots with DeNickey, it can't be good."

Silence rested between them despite the noise from the inmates yelling in the background. Selena shrugged her shoulders and took another sip of her drink.

"I'm not sure how I'd float this job and an undercover job, but until I decide, you'll have to get used to him being around for a while." Selena stood and tossed her empty cup in the gray trash can. Everything was gray around here including Sam's mood.

Sam stood and put his hand on her shoulder. "Be careful. I'm not liking the sound of this."

Selena shrugged his hand off and left to complete her interviews, her emotions twisting in her head.

7

"How do we always meet up like this?" Jeremy flashed his badge at the gym attendee. Lucky for him, Selena was signed up for the class and looking very good in sweatpants and a form-fitting t-shirt.

"What are you doing here?" Selena flushed.

"Came down to teach the class. Figured you could use some expertise." Jeremy punched her lightly on the shoulder.

"Oh great, you're the instructor?"

"Yes. Is there a problem?" Jeremy stopped before entering the locker rooms.

"No. Don't want to see you get hurt."

"Yeah, see you on the other side, Selena." Jeremy laughed. It was the first time he'd used her given name since their eating contest and the corners of his mouth turned up, remembering what a challenge it was to get her to concede to that level with him.

Her hair, piled high on her head in a wadded ponytail, was enticing, and he hoped he might have another encounter with it. Better get your head in the game and not on her hair.

Heavy gym mats lined the center of the spacious

room. Participants in the class gathered in clusters, dressed down and out of uniform, enjoying a day outside the prison walls.

"Okay, class, grab a partner." Jeremy watched the scramble. "I am Special Agent Jeremy Holtz with the FBI and I'll be your instructor for the day. We'll learn several defensive moves as well as some offensive ones. Listen for my instruction. I'll demonstrate, you'll practice, and then we'll practice more until it's a habit. Ready? Here we go." After warming up, Jeremy led them through several aggressive maneuvers with the optional counter measures. He used different partners each time to emphasize the height or size of the attacker was inconsequential. Circling around the group, he came to Selena and her partner, a tall sergeant with a paunchy middle.

"What's the deal with you two?" Jeremy asked, watching the pair eye each other. He had a feeling Selena's mouth had been running, and the big guy's ego kicked in. Jeremy stepped behind Selena, out of their maneuvering space.

"She's got a smart mouth and can't back up her words."

"Go ahead. Do the defensive move now." Jeremy advised.

The sergeant stepped in as if to punch Selena at the same time Jeremy grabbed a fistful of her hair. Jerked backwards, Selena's surprised yelp brought a slight curve to Jeremy's lips.

"What was that for?" Selena spit out, still tangled in his grasp and tight up against his muscular frame.

"Think. I want you to think. Did you see me standing behind you? You gotta be aware." Jeremy kept his eyes on the sergeant, but alert to what Selena was going to do. He whispered in her ear. "It seems like we've been in this position before." Out loud to the class he said, "Class, what should she do?"

Several of the others gathered around to watch.

Before anyone could respond, Selena flipped around, bent at the waist, and rammed the top of her head into his nose. Jeremy immediately let go of her hair and cradled his face. Bright splats of blood dripped into his hand.

"I am so sorry. I'm really sorry."

"Take ten, everybody." Jeremy tried to control the bleeding. Selena followed him to a bench. A gym attendee handed him ice in a towel. "Thanks."

"Selena, why does someone always get hurt when we play?" He muttered around the cloth pressed on his face.

"I don't know. I don't play well with others?" Selena laid cool fingers over the top of his forehead and a firm hand on the back of his neck, adding her own pressure. He smelled a faint alluring fragrance with her closeness.

"Jeremy, open your eyes." Selena adjusted the towel. "Do you feel okay?"

Jeremy let himself stare into her dark blue ones. They were perfect. The whites around them accented the depth and magnificent range of color from almost black to dark cobalt. Concern accented curvy eyebrows and long lashes.

"Jeremy." Selena pulled the towel away from his nose. "Hey, you're going to have to talk to me."

"You're very pretty, you know?" Jeremy smirked at her.

"I think you've been hit in the head too many times." Selena pulled away from him.

Jeremy turned in the bloody towel and waved off the concern. "Let's do some more maneuvers, and then we'll be done for the day."

~

Selena did the self-defense moves she was instructed and left quickly from the training. What was she thinking smashing his nose like that? And then his crazy ramblings about how pretty she was? He was definitely making fun of her.

Changing quickly into jeans and a clean t-shirt, she pulled her hair back up into a loose ponytail. So done with this day. Selena moved through the locker room and out the door. Unfortunately, Jeremy was waiting for her in the parking lot, leaned up against her Blazer with his athletic legs encased in a worn pair of jeans and water droplets clinging to his hair. He looked pretty good. As she got closer, she could see his bloody t-shirt tied to his gym bag. A pang of guilt swept through her.

Selena remotely unlocked the driver's door, hoping he would move. "I already said I was sorry."

"Yes, but this?" Jeremy held the blood-speckled shirt out to her. "This is going to cost you." His current shirt had "Coke: America's Drink" printed on it and fit as nice as the other one did.

"Ok. Cost me what?"

"Some company time. When we talked last, I asked if we could get together when I was in town next to discuss the undercover gig."

"I didn't hear that."

"Well, I said it, and I'm in town." Jeremy looked away and then back at her. "There are several people going out bowling. We could start there and talk afterwards."

Selena contemplated his offer. He didn't look like he was making fun of her now. He looked genuinely interested.

"Alright. But I throw a mean game." Selena reached around him and ducked inside her Blazer.

"I wouldn't expect anything less." Jeremy muttered.

After confirming the place, she waited for Jeremy to get in his vehicle. Instead of the car or truck she envisioned, he hiked his foot over an all-black motorcycle with tons of chrome. Of course. The good-looking, irritating, I-wanna-slap-the-smirk-off-your-face FBI agent rode a motorcycle, her second favorite thing to ride. First would always be the horses, but motorcycles? They were fun to ride, too.

As she followed him to the bowling alley, she had ample opportunity to admire his assertive mastery of the machine. Plus, the view was nice. His white t-shirt billowed out when he rode on the highway, and Selena watched as his muscular arms with bold, tribal tattoos steered the bike. Reminding herself this was the guy she wanted to hate because of the situations he'd put her in, Selena forced her eyes back to the road and away from the attractive form in front of her.

What if she accepted the undercover gig with him? She'd be his stand-in girlfriend, a role not easy for her to play. Most of the time, he was pushing her buttons, waiting and wanting a reaction. He'd be in her space always. Would his girlfriend live with him, sleep with him? She couldn't do that, pretending or not. He sent her emotions on a roller coaster ride as it was. And was she willing to quit her job for this assignment?

8

Jeremy cut the engine and dropped the kickstand. He loved his bike, loved how it took him out of every situation and gave him a few minutes of uninterrupted peace. The rumble under him caused everything else to drift away. Unfortunately, the attractive Latina in her Blazer behind him was a distraction.

He pulled off his helmet and ran fingers through his curly hair, unsticking it from his head. Sweating in the earlier class workout, it was plastered to his scalp. Not a pretty sight for sure.

Glancing to his right, he watched as Selena freshened her lipstick. She was a beautiful girl, tough, smart, stubborn. Cocky. Again, beautiful. She was quickly becoming his drug of choice each time their paths crossed. His dealings with DeNickey were becoming more concerning the closer he got to Selena. He would have to play his cards right if he wanted to protect her and finish his job.

Jeremy led her to the shoes and then to the row of alleys. He picked one close to the others who had been in the class, but their own private lane.

"Let's see. Whoever gets the first strike, gets to kiss the other." Jeremy laughed and stepped up to the lane.

"Loser." Selena rolled her eyes.

"I can't heeaaar you." Jeremy let the ball loose. It rolled down the gutter. Zero points.

Selena stopped her foot-tapping. "Did you do that on purpose?"

Jeremy gave her a devilish grin. "Why? Did you want me to get a strike?"

"I don't care what you get. I didn't agree to the bet."

"You know, you might not have any control over what I do, or don't do." Jeremy pushed his hand in front of the fan as his ball was returned. He had her on guard, a good place to be. And the flush creeping up her neck meant one of two things, she was going to swing on him if he stepped closer, or she had wanted him to get a strike. Interesting.

After his second ball knocked down only a handful of pins, Selena took her place at the top of the alley. Her first ball down the lane was a straight arrow, plowing into the sweet spot of pins knocking every single one of them over.

"Yes." She pumped an arm in the air.

"Nice."

Jeremy joined her at the end of the lane. With the wooden floor an inch higher than the tiled area he stood on, she could almost look him in the eye. Blocking her way, he studied her face.

"No." Selena shoved him backwards with her fingertips. "Your bet, not mine." She dropped into one of the plastic chairs that surrounded the scoring bench and slipped off her bowling shoes.

"Hey, I'm just teasing you. Come on, you think

you can bowl? Bring it." Jeremy challenged her. He'd almost pushed her too far. Not waiting for a response, he picked up his ball and flung it down the lane. Surprised when most of the pins fell down, he turned and imitated her arm pump. "Yes."

She gave him a cautious smile and slid her bowling shoe back on. "Don't be a loser, and I'll show you how this is done, okay?" Selena rolled her lighter- weight ball in a perfect arc, taking out all but one pin.

Jeremy groaned. "I may be in trouble here."

"You were in trouble before we started bowling."

Eight frames later, Selena won the game with a slight lead. Wiping her nose with a Kleenex, she slipped off the shoes and returned to her tennis shoes she'd worn earlier.

"Allergies?" Jeremy did the same.

"No, smoke. I can't handle much of it. And it gets stuck in my hair for days."

Selena pulled a curl over her shoulder and sniffed it. Grimacing, she stuck her hand out. "Good game, even if you lost."

Jeremy took her hand and held it in his. "Wanna go for a bike ride?" The woman had taken his head off numerous times in the past two weeks, both physically and verbally, and he was asking her to ride his bike with him? He was crazy. Letting go of her hand, he took his shoes up to the return desk and slid on his jacket.

"Only if I can drive it." Selena smiled, her palm out for the keys.

"Uh, no. Not a chance." Jeremy held the door

open for her and took a breath of clean air. "Yes or no?" Unbuckling the helmet from its resting place, Jeremy offered it to her.

"Where's your helmet?" Selena pulled the protective gear onto her head in response.

Jeremy paused. The tight helmet curved her face, forcing strands of hair out from underneath on both sides. "Let me do this." Jeremy slid his fingers up her jaw line and laced the straps about her chin.

"I can ride without one in Oklahoma. I do usually wear one, but I'll make an exception tonight." Pulling the bike off the kickstand, Jeremy motioned for her to get on behind him.

~

Winding through narrow roads away from the bowling alley, the Harley's loud bass reverberated through the countryside. Selena, hands loosely clasped around his middle, laid the face shield of her helmet on his back. The wind swooping over his shoulder missed her protected face but raised the stray ends of her hair peeking out from under the hard plastic riding gear. To her left, farms and pastures flew by. Selena smiled as she thought about what her Papá would say if he could see her. He wouldn't be happy. He always said motorcycles were dangerous.

Thoughts of her father made sudden tears spring up. She hadn't been to see him in several months. How different life was here than at home in Texas.

"Where are we going?" Selena felt the motorcycle gear down.

Turning into a park, Jeremy guided the bike to a stop. "You know, we've battled from day one. I just thought we could sit and enjoy the night air a little."

Sliding off without bumping her with his boot, he leaned up against a low concrete wall dividing the paved road from the grassy playground area. "Is this okay?"

Selena shrugged and stayed on the bike. He'd taken the key out, she noticed. Good for him, he shouldn't trust her an inch. Right now, she didn't think she could trust herself as a breeze blew a whiff of his cologne her direction. She might end up actually liking the guy. Selena stretched her legs out to the front foot pedals and pulled off the helmet, catching her curls in the straps.

Dang it. Her hair caught in everything, the seatbelt, her purse strap, even the ficus tree in her living room.

"Need help?" Jeremy asked.

"No." A little more explosive than she'd like, but his touch was making her shiver. Basta. The man was irritating. Irritatingly good-looking, irritatingly strong, an irritatingly perfect bantering partner.

Selena remained on the bike, adjusting to see him. It was a beautiful night, far away from the smoky bowling alley and the stressful prison.

"Hey, come on, I want to show you something." Jeremy hopped over the wall and moved to the low flat building with two grills for cooking outside and picnic benches on either side. Dim lighting illuminated the picnic area. On the side of the building, a small ladder led to the roof.

"Oh, uh-uh. I'm not going up there." Selena shook her head. Heights were the worst. A spinning sensation would start in her head and stir up her stomach until she was sick and near vomiting.

"It's not high. You can see the stars better up here." Jeremy had already started the climb. "Seriously, just try. Scaredy cat."

"Shut up." Selena grasped the lower rung. "This better be worth it." She muttered. Why was she following this guy? After all that had happened between them, he was probably scheming how to throw her over. Pulling herself over the top, she found Jeremy sitting in the center of the roof, cross-legged. Lowering next to him, "Okay, what?"

"Look up." Jeremy pointed.

The expanse of the sky unfolded above her. Tiny lights twinkled from the universe, begging her to pick out the uniform constellations.

"Sweet." Selena whispered. This was beautiful, peaceful, restful. Usually guarded, Selena blinked away tired tears.

"Why so quiet?" Jeremy pressed.

Selena swiped at her eyes. She would not cry. She would not, she would not.

"Just tired. Thinking about my father. Glad to be out and away for a change." Selena cast a sidelong look at him. "Even if it's with you."

"Ha, ha. You wouldn't be here if it wasn't for me." Jeremy reached out and pulled a curl.

"Stop it." Selena moved out of his grasp.

Jeremy laughed, a rich tone laced with humor. She enjoyed listening to him chuckle.

"Tell me about your father." Jeremy picked up a rock and tossed it over the side.

"He's the lead man on a huge cattle ranch in Texas, near the Mexico border. My mother, Susannah, died during childbirth with my younger brother, in Mexico. I was only four. Thinking he could find better work in Texas, he picked up and left with me."

"Did he find that to be the case?" Jeremy chucked more pebbles off the roof.

"Yeah, he was passing by a small herd of cattle tangled in barbed wire, stopped to get them out and ran them to the rancher up the road. The rancher kept him on, and he's been there ever since." Selena picked up her own rock and rubbed her thumb over the flat side. "The housekeeper there kinda took me in, really adopted me. She always says, 'Laughter is good medicine. If you can laugh, you can live.'"

"Sounds cool."

"The ranch is. Missing my father isn't."

"Sorry."

~

Jeremy watched her out of half-closed eyes, thinking of his own history. The motorcycles had been a draw for him. Recruited by the FBI as a young law enforcement officer, Jeremy had taken every opportunity to slide motorcycles into his life. Working undercover for almost two years in a motorcycle gang, Jeremy sometimes forgot he was FBI and just enjoyed their companionship. He'd actually come to a point where he liked some of them, or at least understood them. Growing a beard, getting scruffy, and custom building his own motorcycle was a small part of the job. Finding a close spot to the inner workings of the group wasn't as hard as fighting emotionally to stay disconnected from them. Many were family men, albeit rough ones, and playing the part of a loyal friend was difficult. Often, he wondered if he was losing his own personality in the creation of the brooding, radical biker persona he had created.

Selena interrupted his thoughts. "Tell me more about this girlfriend thing."

Ah, yes, the girlfriend thing. Jeremy threw a pebble at a spot on the roof, making a bulls-eye target. Jeremy looked back at Selena. The pale moonlight created paths of silken rain falling from the top of her head, curls brushing the bottom of her chin. Her eyes were dark. How did he explain the girlfriend thing without giving away too much information?

"Well, it's not really a girlfriend thing. Or it is, but short term." Jeremy sighed. "I got hooked up with these guys a couple of years ago on an undercover job. When I left, left the undercover position, I told them I got a girl pregnant, and she was pushing me to get married. I needed an excuse to get out. They were mostly guys with family, so my attempt at being an upstanding citizen worked with them."

Selena slanted a look at him. "Upstanding? Really?"

"Never been undercover, huh? Look, the job required me to spend a lot of time with them. I played ball on their softball team, I played pool at their house, sometimes, I even dated their cousin."

"Sounds like you had it rough." She chuckled, throwing her own rock at the imaginary target, landing close to his.

"It is when you know you are eventually going to have to flip them, and they'll be taken away from their kids and wives."

"True. Why their group?"

"A little drug stuff going on. Nothing serious with them but we were looking at suppliers in their area and the best way to infiltrate them." Jeremy explained, downplaying the extent of the operation or that he was still connected to them in a non-professional capacity.

"Are you going back under? The reason you need a girlfriend?" Selena asked.

"Maybe. Didn't want to blow my cover so I need to bring the girlfriend back." Jeremy launched another rock, chipping Selena's out farther.

"Hey." Selena searched for another piece of gravel. Flipping it around in her hand, she moved to a different angle. Her rock hit his, shattering it. "Yes." she jumped up, clapping her hands.

"I don't think you were aiming at the target. I think you were just trying to knock me out of the game." Jeremy pretended to pout, standing with her.

Once again, they were competing, safe ground.

~

Selena sucked in a breath and held it until she caught Jeremy staring at her.

"What are you doing?" He stepped in front of her, causing her to choose. Step back and she'd be giving in, step forward and they'd be nose-to-nose. One was obviously more appealing than the other, but neither was going to happen.

"Nothing. Shut up and throw. Oh wait, there's nothing left of your rock. Nothing to aim for." Selena could smell the butterscotch candy he had sucked on earlier. It had been a long day. His nearness was making her light-headed.

"You were holding your breath. Why?"

"I hold my breath when I'm having a good time, okay?" Selena said, eyes never breaking contact with his.

"What?"

"If you say I'm weird, I'm going to throat punch you."

"Not weird," He blocked a playful punch. "Well, okay, yeah, weird is the word."

"It is not." Selena attempted another punch, one not as light. Caught, his hands gently wrapped around her wrists. "I told you why, now let go."

"Why again?"

"I hold my breath when I'm having a good time because I think if you hold your breath, time stops moving, and you can enjoy the time." Selena ran her words together as she moved away from his touch.

"It also makes your chest all blotchy," He pointed at the redness creeping up her neck, visible only by the moonlight.

"Thanks." Selena sat down, cautiously, as Jeremy sat, too, on a side wall toward the center of the roof.

Jeremy pointed at a star shooting off to the right. "Do you believe in God?"

"Yes."

"I believe in God. I also believe in Nature and the power of you and the power in me."

"But not God."

"Yes, I believe there is a God. Not one that has power in this world like other people believe. I believe God spoke to all of those old guys although

I struggle with the concept of a Garden of Eden. I think it may be more hypothetical than real. I believe God created man with a free will, and we now choose how we want our lives to go. God has very little to do with me or how I run my life. I believe I live my life in freedom without the restraints or laws God gave men a thousand years ago."

Selena lifted her face to the sky.

"Freedom, an interesting choice of words. I've never thought about God and freedom that way."

"I think freedom describes my view on religion. It's my opportunity to take what I believe about myself and run with it. I have the power. In me."

"A little passionate about all this, aren't you?" Selena turned her full gaze on him.

"When I was young, I was the runt of the pack. I didn't have any self-esteem. I was a loser. Then, an uncle came along, took the place of my worthless father, and showed me how powerful I could really be. I love freedom and I love the power it creates."

"Wow. You sound so patriotic. Just kidding. Sounds like someone gave you a good turn. Why you can relate to the gang guys. You know how they feel and how they could feel." Selena put her hand on his arm. Lightening zinged in her fingertip capillaries all the way up to the bigger veins. Snatching her hand away, she said, "Pretty cool."

"Race ya to the bike." Jeremy leaped for the wall ladder.

Good. Competition again. Nice, safe competition.

9

Selena and Sam sat in the Receiving Office on Monday afternoon, working quickly to prepare for the arrival of new inmates. In a companionable rhythm, Selena inspected the files, passed them on to Sam, who made room assignments and completed paperwork.

"Most of these guys have over 100 years to serve. They're way out of our security range." Selena wound an abstract curl around her finger.

"Yeah, I know, but we agreed to take them."

Selena shook her head at the information she was reading in the files.

"Why though?"

"Money. Isn't that where everything leads? The other states pay to put their inmates in our prison, lots of it." Sam pushed the paperwork into a manila envelope. "Meet me back here at 8 pm, and we'll suit up. You get to go with us on this trip. Picking up inmates at the airport should be an experience for you."

~

"You ready?" Sam asked, handing her a black cap with Corrections printed on it in gold letters.

"Yes." Selena felt the churning in her stomach. Usually, only transportation guards were allowed to go on these missions. Dressed all in black, Selena wadded up her hair and pushed it into the cap.

Sam put on his windbreaker and headed up the stairs. Several men spilled out of the armory room. Handing out large weapons and ammunition belts, the captain of the Elite Emergency Squad assessed her. With a quick nod, he turned and gave directions to his men.

"The flights from Chicago and D.C. are expected to land in an hour. There are twelve of us, four to each bus. We're not expecting trouble, but ready if need be. Stay alert. These inmates are not going to be happy about landing in Oklahoma." The captain grinned.

Loading up, Selena rode in front of the metal grid separating inmates from guards and braced for the bumpy bus ride.

"This is like an episode of Rambo." She whispered to Sam.

"How so?"

"The E-squad with their big guns and ammunition. It's like a combat zone."

Reaching the destination, guards spilled out of the buses and lined up quietly, side by side. A soft breeze blew over the tarmac belying the heavy tension in the air. Each guard held a weapon at the ready, tense and alert, all eyes on the plane.

Selena stood by the bus she had ridden in and waited with the guards. Slowly, the door hatch opened, and the first inmates shuffled down the steps. Cuffed at the wrists and the ankles with a belly chain ensuring safety, one by one they left the plane. Selena mentally counted the displaced inmates as they stumbled between the heavily armed guards, forty-three from D.C. and fifty-seven from Chicago.

A skirmish at one of the bus doors brought several guards running. They wrestled the inmate to the ground, using a taser gun to subdue him.

"What happened?" The captain stepped to the side as two guards tossed the inmate to a seat.

"He decided to be ornery. Looks like he was the same on the plane here. He's got numerous taser bruises on him."

"Well, watch him and take of it if he decides to be stupid again."

The convoy of buses finished loading and made their way back to the prison. Selena turned halfway in her seat when she heard one of the inmates cursing loudly. "We're in Oklahoma? Home of the Cow Pies?" he shouted.

"Welcome to Oklahoma, boys." Sam smiled at her from the next seat. The remaining twenty-minute ride flew by despite the disgruntled inmates behind her. Soon, they were in the port of the building and preparing to unload. Selena breathed out the tension as she and Sam headed downstairs to the investigator's office.

Beside her desk, Sam took a deep breath himself. "I always hold my breath during those things. It's like if I don't breathe, nothing bad will happen."

Selena smiled at him and picked up the files on each delivered inmate. They had their own reasons for holding their breath. Selena smiled again at the time spent with Jeremy. "There's still work to do."

"Yeah, but they're on my turf now."

With their corrections windbreakers on and a group of ten inmates following in orange jumpsuits, Sam and Selena led them down to Housing Unit #1.

Brandon, Sam's clerk, stood in the doorway of Sam's office watching the inmates arrive.

"Let's close up shop and do the rest of the paperwork in the morning. A bunch of us are going to the "Hole in the Wall" to blow off steam. Want to go?"

"Sure. Better than going home. I'm still all jacked up about bringing those inmates in." Selena slid out of her windbreaker and shook out her hair from the cap. "I'll meet you there."

~

Sam set drinks in front of the empty chair next to Selena. She accepted her diet Coke, thanking him. Never having been a drinker, she declined alcohol, but not an invitation to the party.

"Mind if we sit with you?" A captain and an officer stood at their table. Sam nodded at the empty chairs.

"Hear you brought in a plane load tonight." The stout police officer glanced from Selena to Sam and back.

"Yeah." Sam agreed.

"Lose any of them?"

"Nope. That's your job." They bantered as Selena assessed the bar scene. Most of the bar clientele were law enforcement with a few women who stood out in their frilly short skirts and exposed chests. Selena thought they looked desperate in an after-midnight way. For all she knew, they could be wives or hookers or both. Selena looked down at her own black, rumpled outfit. She hadn't bothered with a change in clothes.

"Hey, isn't DeNickey over there?" Sam nudged her with his elbow.

Following his line of sight, Selena looked over at a corner of the bar. With a scantily dressed woman hanging on his shoulder, DeNickey's rotund form was recognizable even from the back. As she scanned the crowd he was with, Selena noticed Jeremy, also with his back to her. Jeremy turned toward the bar and absently caught her eye. She suppressed her surprise as he approached their table.

"Well, look who it is," Sam muttered under his breath.

Selena quickly searched his eyes before turning to greet Jeremy.

"Hey, aren't you out a little late?" Jeremy's taunting voice wafted over her as he shook hands with the others at their table. "Sam."

"Shouldn't you be turning into a pumpkin about now? Squash?" Disrespect colored Sam's voice.

"Nah, just came in for a drink." Jeremy leaned his long fingers on the table, in a patronizing way. "Hey, Selena, I've got a table right over there." Jeremy indicated where DeNickey was seated.

"Sure. I've only got a couple of minutes, though, and then I'll be the one turning into a pumpkin." Selena tapped Sam on the shoulder, said goodnight to the others and followed Jeremy to his table. She'd have to ask Sam later why the evil eye on Jeremy. She didn't think they knew each other from the conversation she and Sam had had earlier.

"Jeremy," Selena touched his arm, stopping him before arriving at the table. "Do you know Sam?"

"Just of him." Jeremy shook his head, taking her hand in his.

"Hey, wait." Selena pulled away from him. "I don't want to sit with DeNickey. If you want to, go ahead, but I'm not interested." This is what kept DeNickey away from his job this evening? Selena was thrilled for the opportunity to go to the transport plane but somehow finding out DeNickey's important business was at a bar didn't sit well.

Despite her objections, Jeremy continued to the table. "He's harmless. You'll be fine."

As he turned and spoke to her, she could smell the alcohol on his breath. She was probably the exception, the only one not drinking besides Sam. Selena followed. Sitting across from her supervisor, Selena greeted the buxom blonde hanging on DeNickey. The girl could barely put two words together. She seemed to be missing part of her brain as well as her shirt. She was definitely not hiding her intentions, or anything else, very well.

"Well, well. Interesting to see you here. In a place like this. With married men like him." DeNickey hooked a thumb at Sam, still sitting with the captain and guard. Why did he always have to make her feel like dirt? DeNickey could make a rose stink.

Selena stood when DeNickey offered to get another round of drinks. Finally. Now's the time to go. The other three were getting drunker by the minute.

"Listen, I'd better get going. I still have to work in the morning." She glanced over at Sam's table only to find he had already left. Selena scooted around Jeremy and slipped out of a sloppy embrace. Not attractive, Mr. FBI.

"Going so soon?" DeNickey said, sidled up to her and put his arm around her waist.

Selena stepped away from him. Sick man. She'd like to drop him to the floor with a good swift kick.

"See ya tomorrow, then." DeNickey clasped her shoulder.

Selena pulled out of his grip. Pushing through the door, she felt the cool outdoor air on her face and took a deep breath. She'd lay awake tonight thinking of all the horrible things she'd like to do to the man who was her boss.

10

Good. Lights out. He was probably sleeping off his hangover. Selena passed DeNickey's door on the way to her office the next day. The time went much quicker when she didn't have to be alert to his next purposeful brush against her or sick comment.

Brandon, Sam's inmate clerk, waited beside the outer door.

"What are you doing here?" Selena unlocked the door for him and set her briefcase against the wall behind her desk.

He handed her a bulging communications envelope. "Mr. Matthews sent this." He looked at his black, inmate-issued boots, not meeting her eyes. "And he said you might be able to use my help later."

Taking the envelope, Selena untied the top and pulled out a warm diet soda. Laughing, she set it on her coaster and scrawled out a "Thank you" and gave the envelope back. Sam always knew how to brighten her day.

Selena watched Brandon walk towards the correct housing unit, envelope swinging in his hand. She speculated what he was in for. Theft? Drugs? Murder? She'd have to check his file. Sam liked him, but Sam didn't really care what they were in prison for. She did. What crime they committed said a lot about a person. She continued to watch his confident gait, coal hair shining in the sun, until he was lost in the overhang of the building. He was a nice-looking inmate, respectful. His type had caused more than one civilian at the prison to lose their job. The nice ones tugged at heart strings and conned their way into illegal favors. Brandon didn't seem to be one of those. Maybe he truly was nice. Selena sighed. But why did they have to look good? Untouchable, yet handsome.

~

Brandon followed the obligatory protocol for making a phone call. "Hey, I'm in. Matthews recommended I run for Maldanado. I guess she thought Matthews' word was enough." It felt good to hear Suzie's voice. The assigned four walls they called his living quarters were lonely. Suzie grounded him, gave him the key to the outside world if only for a little while. One foot in the prison culture and one big toe still connected to the outside, that's how he'd survive. Not like his cellmate who'd completely submerged himself in prison, living out his life lifting weights, playing basketball, and the occasional fight. Everyone watched everyone though, and Brandon found it exhausting. "Step Two, I guess, huh?"

Brandon could hear Suzie smacking gum on the other side of the line. Watermelon flavored would be awesome. He could almost smell it.

Small chitchat with Suzie was just what he needed. He listened to her talk about unimportant things, enjoying those unimportant things.

"Hey, Suz. Take a breath." Brandon stopped her chatter. No noise on the yard. No yelling, no weights clanging. Brandon chanced a look over his shoulder and felt the tension. No one was moving, even the wind seemed to take a break. "I gotta go, something's up. I'll call you later."

"Wait, can I come visit soon?"

"Yeah, yeah. I gotta go. Bye." Brandon hung up the phone, listening with every muscle to the vibrations in the yard. Turning around, the only movement he saw was Maldanado walking down the sidewalk, head down, files in hand. Why wasn't she looking around? Couldn't she sense the tension? Something was up and it was physical and pulsating, ready to explode. Brandon watched her walk farther until she was in front of the Hole. Glancing around, trying to decipher where the danger lay, he moved quickly down the fence line and into the shady area in front of the housing unit.

~

Selena felt more than saw the charge from the gymnasium. Instinctively, she quickened her pace. Feeling relatively safer under the awning of Sam's housing unit, she allowed her gaze to follow the movement across the yard.

Two inmates rushed out of the gym, one with a heavy sock in his hand chasing the other. Cursing each other, the men circled around, now surrounded by anyone who was out on the yard. Guards ran from every direction, talking sideways into their radios, calling for backup. Selena watched as one of the fighters was tossed a knife, a homemade "shank", from someone in the outer circle. The nearest white shirt officer slid to a stop outside the writhing circle of inmates. Who knew how many weapons were among them? Most all had some type, whether it be a toothbrush whittled sharp or a piece of metal busted from their bunk beds. There were no fair fights in prison. This open display of aggression was abnormal, though. Most inmates preferred for there to be few witnesses. A stab in the back passing through the lunch line was better than everyone in the yard seeing what took place and being able to name names.

Selena watched the guards try to control the situation.

"You need to get in the house, Ma'am." a voice whispered in her ear. Selena's heart raced. She could feel his breath, could see the grey pants out of the corner of her eye. Fear enveloped her as she realized an inmate stood directly behind her, close enough to whisper in her ear.

Selena whirled around to the voice. "Brandon. Inmate Rollos." She let out a breath and glanced at him. He looked at her, eye to eye, not like the downward stare from before.

"You really need to get inside." He put his hands in his pockets and glanced slowly left and then to the right. "Mr. Matthews is there."

Selena fled through the doors, sweat slithering down her back. Looking back once, she saw Brandon slide back into the shadows of the awning. "Sam. Sam. There's a fight on the yard!"

Sam rushed at her from the back office. "Come on, it's safest in the bubble."

Through the airlock and up with the other officers, Selena allowed herself to take deep breaths. Fights weren't uncommon on the yard but Brandon standing behind her had been frightening.

Watching as the yard officers ended the fight with tear gas and taser guns, she heard Sam make arrangements and set up rooms for the fighters in the locked down unit.

Once completed, she followed Sam back to his office where he pulled the ever-present Diet Coke out of a drawer.

"Where were you when it started?

"On my way down here to have an inmate sign his statement. The fight didn't shake me. Your clerk did." Selena put her hands on her hips. "He scared the spit out of me."

"How?"

"He came up behind me and whispered in my ear while I was watching the fight. I don't think he can work for me."

"Wait," Sam picked up the phone and called the bubble. "Hey, if you see Inmate Rollos out front can you send him back? I'll be up later to help with the fighters."

Selena stared at him. "What are you going to say? Don't scare her next time? Don't whisper in her ear? Come on, Sam."

"Yes, sir?" Brandon materialized at the door.

"Hey, any reason for you to…"

"I'll handle this," Selena hooked her chin up and peered down at the inmate. No way was she allowing Sam to chastise an inmate on her behalf. "I was talking to Mr. Matthews about writing you up for inappropriate behavior with a staff person."

Brandon cringed. "I apologize if it looked that way. Not how I meant it."

Selena softened as she heard sincerity in his voice. "What did you mean?"

"I know you could have been a prime target, standing out in the yard, watching something else take place, and not aware of anything behind you. I wanted you to get inside before anyone else thought the same thing."

"Really." Selena tapped her fingernails on Sam's desk. "I'm supposed to believe you thought you were protecting me? Do I look like I need protection?"

"Yes, ma'am… I mean, no, ma'am."

"You're dismissed." Selena slouched into a plastic office chair. She craned her neck around to see if Brandon was out of hearing range. "What do you think?"

"I think I believe him. You could have been a prime target. You know, create a scene over there, something different happens over here. A diversion. Maybe he was." Sam shrugged his shoulders. "It's possible."

"I don't like it." An inmate protecting her from possible harm? Enough foresight to see she could be in trouble and to warn her? Any one of the guards would have done the same thing, protected her, but an inmate? Maybe he was just nice. Doubtful, but maybe.

Selena rose from her chair. "Hey, are you coming tonight? You know, poker night? It's the first Friday of the month."

"Think you'll win this time? Ms. Card Shark. I'm always in." Sam paused. "Your FBI boyfriend coming?"

"Well, I wouldn't exactly call him my boyfriend, but I think he is. Hey, that brings up a good question. Do you know him?" Selena brought up Sam and Jeremy's interaction at the bar.

"A little. I've seen his work a few times." Sam shrugged, staring intently at her. "Didn't realize your Jeremy was 'that Jeremy' until the night at the bar."

Selena dismissed the intimate "your Jeremy" comment. A conversation for another day.

~

"Okay, ante up." One of the guards motioned with his coins.

Selena glanced at the microwave clock. 2:00 a.m. "Nope, I'm out. I got nothing." Selena tossed her cards in.

Walking into the large open front room, she expected to see Jeremy slumped in the recliner, off in wonder-wonder land. Jeremy was the only one not playing cards with the other five guys still around her dining table. Sam had made his exit hours ago in time to put his kids to bed. There had been little interaction between Sam and Jeremy, just an uncomfortable avoidance.

Where was Jeremy? Not in the recliner and not in the kitchen. Surely, he hadn't left without saying anything. She knew as an agent, there would be times when he left unexpectedly or for periods of time, but she'd hoped he might leave a note or something.

Standing still in the glow of the moon shining in the window, she heard a voice on the front porch.

Was Jeremy out there talking to someone?

Selena tiptoed to the open screen door and listened for the voice again. It was Jeremy but it looked like he was talking on his cell phone, not to a person.

"Yeah, I'm here." Jeremy breathed into his phone.

Selena stepped to the side of the door.

"I know, I know. We're getting there. She'll have to trust me first and then I'll ask her." Jeremy's voice hushed as he turned away from the door and walked farther from the house. She could barely see his shape in the shadow of her Blazer.

"Jeremy, is everything alright?" Selena called to him as she quietly closed the door behind her. There was something that made her uneasy about his phone call. Nothing specific, just uneasy.

Quickly turning toward her and putting his phone in his pocket, he said, "Looking for your snorer."

"My what?"

"Snorer…I heard someone snoring out in your yard."

She walked toward him and stopped, listening. There was a distinct snoring sound out in the yard. Crooking a finger at him, Selena made her way by moonlight to a corner of the barn.

"I think I found him." Propped up in his jeans and ragged T-shirt, Doug sat snoring contently. "I thought he left hours ago."

"He's going to hurt in the morning, sitting on the ground."

"Should we leave him?"

"I would. He'll be okay."

"He must have added something to his drink. He wasn't drinking inside." Selena leaned down and smelled his breath. "Definitely Tequila."

Jeremy took her hand and pulled her to the porch swing. Leaning his head back and pushing gently with his toe, Jeremy kept her hand in his. She debated taking it back.

"Who was the phone call from?" Selena struggled to remember why she'd come outside in the first place as he stroked his thumb across her palm.

"Business." Jeremy glanced at her. "I kinda like this."

"Like what?" Selena resisted the urge to lean in to him.

"Not fighting. Not getting the snot beat out of me or having a gun put in my face." Jeremy smiled.

"You mean, by me. I think you deserved most of it."

"Yeah, well, I could get used to a little less of that and a little more of this." Jeremy dropped her hand and put his arm around the back of the swing. "Come on, just relax for a bit."

Selena closed her eyes and settled back against his muscular arm. She could get used to this, too.

11

Eyes tired from the weekend, Selena walked through the gate and listened for the tell-tale click behind her, the relocking of the gate. The inmates hated the sound; the guards lived for it.

Selena passed one of the picnic tables on the yard and saw Brandon sitting alone, reading. After the last incident where she'd put him in his place, he hadn't been around much.

Curious, she stopped. "What are you reading?" She expected him to say *Unfair Treatment of Inmates*, although his behavior hadn't led her to believe he thought that way. She couldn't shake the concern he'd sparked in her after his whispered suggestion she move to a more protected place. And yet, she was touched, too, that he valued her safety.

"The Bible." Brandon glanced up.

His eyes were unexpectedly blue. With his Native American coloring, she thought they would be brown.

He hesitated before looking back at the tattered pages. "Did you need me this morning?"

"No. Why are you reading the Bible?" It seemed sacrilegious, an inmate reading the Bible. Everyone knew jailhouse religion was pretend.

"Do you mean, am I one of those inmates who finds God after he's killed eleven people and now shouldn't deserve the death penalty?"

Selena narrowed her eyes. He'd killed eleven people? Who was this guy? A lot of inmates found God as an escape from the consequences of their actions. There were never any changes in their lives, they went on leading their lives as before.

Her Papá had encountered God after meeting Jolie on the ranch. They both claimed to be Christians now, although her father was a good person before finding God. Afterwards, he hadn't changed except to follow Jolie's religious practices. He was still a good man. Jeremy's views made more sense, God may have been relevant in ancient times, but it was up to her to make things happen in her life. The power lay in her alone.

Selena startled as Inmate Rollos cleared his voice. She'd stood in the same place for how long?

"I haven't killed eleven people if that's what you're thinking. Just four." Brandon smiled at the ground. Apparently, the eye contact was over.

"Not very funny in a place like this."

"You're right. I'm sorry. Out of line."

"Uh, huh. Seems to be a lot of that going around." Selena adjusted her backpack. Sam always treated inmates like the people they were, until they weren't. "Listen, I may have been too hard on you when the fight broke out. But, well, Sam says your intentions were good, and I may have overreacted. I won't apologize or give any thanks, so, well, there's that. Not in a habit of doing that with anyone." Selena stopped, realizing she was rambling, to an inmate, of all people. "Come around in an hour and I'll find something for you to do."

"Yes, ma'am."

~

Brandon watched Maldanado continue across the yard. He could hear her heels clicking on the sidewalk. He often saw a softer side to her, which didn't gel with her hard, outer shell. Like now, she seemed truly interested in what he was reading and why it was the Bible. Brandon gazed off in the distance. He was making a way for her to be something that didn't line up with the facts. The facts were she may have ties to the drugs inside the prison. She was very pretty, a strong Latina, and they could have been friends on the outside. Could they have been friends? He'd wanted to protect her earlier when the fight broke out. And just now, he'd really wanted her to see him as something other than a convict. He'd blown it when he mentioned killing people. She may have let her guard down a little until he said that.

For Pete's sake. Brandon shook his head. He was an inmate; she was his authority. What was he thinking? He could never disrespect her by thinking anything else. Inmate, Corrections staff. Brandon, Maldanado. And yet, he let his thoughts wander about the 'what ifs'.

Maldanado thought he'd killed eleven people? He'd been honest about the four, although she would never know. It wasn't in his jacket file because he'd never been convicted. Made the newspaper but not the court system and never with his right name.

Returning his Bible to the cell, he paced the yard for a few minutes before hearing his name called over the loudspeaker.

"Inmate Brandon Rollos. To the Visiting Room. You have a visitor."

Brandon hurried down the sidewalk to the gate with access to the visiting area. A young, shiny-faced guard patted him down as he tried to crane his neck around the last of the corners. After a tap on the wall where the visiting rules hung in 5-inch print, the officer released him through a heavy, locked door. Brandon hurried into the large, dingy room where twenty other guys met with their visitors.

Standing at the doorway on the other side, Suzie waited for him. Brandon crossed to her quickly.

"We can sit over here." He led her over to an empty set of chairs.

"I can honestly say this is one place I have never been. I've been a lot of places but…" Suzie's voice drifted off as she looked around the room. Veneer-chipped tables sat against the wall; most of the chairs filled with inmates and their guests. Some of the conversations were loud and obnoxious, others were hushed.

"I'm sorry I'm here but glad you came." Brandon drummed his fingers on the table.

Suzie smiled, a glint of humor in her eyes. "The poor boy routine won't work on me," She tossed long, golden hair over her shoulder. Brandon caught one of the other inmate's looks as he watched Suzie, too. Even the guards were ogling her.

"Suzie…" Brandon gritted his teeth. "You've got to lay low. For all this to work, you've got to be in the background. Unmemorable. Please."

"Did you just call me 'unremarkable'?"

"No. Unmemorable. Come on, work with me here. There is no way you could be unremarkable." Brandon whispered.

"I'm messing with you. Next time, I'll come without makeup, looking like a bag lady."

Brandon groaned. Suzie knew how to lay low. They'd done it numerous times together. It didn't take much for her to decide she wanted to be the center of attention and then Brandon wanted to throttle her. And she could never look like a bag lady. With honey colored hair and soft brown eyes, her face alone turned heads. Add a curvaceous figure and she was destined to gain interest from the males around her.

"Do I look different?" Brandon ran his palm over his sparse beard, a newly acquired look.

"The beard makes you look a little scruffy. I personally like you a little . . . cleaner." Suzie shrugged and glanced around the room. "Not great company."

"No." Brandon looked around his surroundings. He and Suzie had been in rough neighborhoods together and with some even rougher people.

"Hey, what are you thinking about?"

Brandon brought his focus back to Suzie. "God, amazingly enough. How he brought me to this point in my life. How looking at me...or any of these guys...and you'd think society wished we'd disappear or suffer evil, horrible repercussions. But many of these guys have good hearts, just a string of bad choices." He was also thinking about

Maldanado, what she thought of him.

"I know where you're going with this, but you put yourself here. They put themselves here, albeit for different reasons. God didn't have a lot to do with it." Suzie always rolled her eyes at his Christianity talk even when he wasn't incarcerated.

"Suz, you know I'm not a bad guy. You know my heart's good." Brandon leaned as close as he could and kept eye contact with her.

"I know why you're in here, and it's NOT like the others."

"Hey, have I told you lately, how much I appreciate you? I know this is a lot different than what we've ever done together before, but I'd be remiss if I didn't tell you. It's killing me not to bounce stuff off you whenever I want. I know this is a job, but it's really wearing on me. Having you visit reminds me I'm not who these people think I am."

"I will never blow your cover. You will always be my partner whether separated by bars or sitting next to me in the squad car. This will be over soon, and we'll go back to our normal lives."

Brandon knew all of that. And he'd been in undercover positions before, but prison was dark, and he'd always treasured his ability to live with integrity as much as the job would allow. Jail meant thinking like the con men he found himself surrounded by, not his vibe at all.

"Okay, okay. Let's talk about something else. Tell me what's happening at the shop."

"Well, Manny started a Saturday evening poker game. I'm not sure if it's on the up-and-up since I don't see any of the money coming through the shop.

He must be getting cash another way. They sure don't play for pennies. Speaking of which, your investigator lady you wanted information on, also has a poker game at her house. Have you heard that yet?"

"Good to know. Who's it with? Guards?" Brandon looked over his shoulder at the guards.

"Yeah, with guards and there's an FBI agent sniffing around, too. Can't imagine what the attraction is with her." Suzie picked at her fingernails.

"Are you kidding me? Have you seen her? She's a beautiful girl; should never be working in a place like this. They'll eat her alive in a year."

"I think she's been here longer now. So, you think she's beautiful? Don't you dare go that direction." Suzie cautioned.

"Don't get all motherly on me. I know what I'm doing."

"Please, please, don't do anything stupid."

"New topic. Suz, you have to trust me. Really." Brandon's eyes begged her to believe him.

12

"Jolie, cómo estás?" Selena moved her cell phone to her other ear. Listening to the excited chatter in Spanish, Selena put her feet up on her desk. Selena knew better than to interrupt, so she just nodded her head, allowing thoughts of home to wash over her. The last time she had gone home, she helped the ranch hands with a community event, "The Great American Shootout", a cowboy action shooting competition.

Riding horses since she was little and trained to shoot straight, Selena loved competing in the event. Wearing a deerskin outfit with fringe on the cuffs and skirt, Selena rode her horse, She'Daisy in the full, competition-required attire. Jolie had coined her "Sweet Seat Sally" as an 1800's nickname, and it had stuck. The frilly name made her ears turn a little pink, but she endured the jesting and rode to perfection almost every time.

Finding a break in the conversation, Selena finally asked, "How's Papá?"

"Your padre is buen. He's getting ready for the Shootout. Will you be home?" Jolie's switch back and forth from Spanish to English was always endearing.

"I'm not sure. Let me check things out here and get back with you."

"Okay, Adiós, Cuidate." Goodbye, take care.

Selena looked up to see Brandon standing at the locked door. Putting her cell phone away in her purse, she stepped over to the door and pushed the release bar.

"I was on my way back from the visiting room and thought I'd stop by to see if you had any work ready." Brandon glanced at the clock on the wall, back to Selena, and then to the floor.

"Who was the visit with?" There was something about this guy that intrigued her. He was respectful enough, despite his admission to having killed four people. She really needed to check his file. He had to be exaggerating.

"My girlfriend." Brandon continued looking at the floor. "She doesn't get up this way often."

"Really? Where does she live?" Girlfriend? Interesting. What type of woman would knowingly date a guy who had killed four people? Of course, there were women who thought inmates were appealing. Maybe he protected her, too? Selena shook her head, as if trying to shake her thoughts right out onto the ground. What did she care?

"In Texas. Where I'm from."

Selena studied him for a minute. "Let me get some things together and then you can run them for me." She rifled through the paperwork on her desk. "Do you know anyone from this group?" Selena pushed a single paper across her desk. A list of known gang leaders was written in capital letters in the center of the page.

"They say they're religious." Selena shrugged. "You're religious."

"I am a Christian, which doesn't always equate with religion. Or what these guys term as religion." Brandon looked up at her. "I believe in God and faith and freedom. These guys believe they are gods and have faith in themselves and believe more in controlling others than freedom for all. They talk about freedom, but they don't really know what freedom is."

"Tell me what freedom is, then." Selena leaned back in her chair. Another discussion on freedom. First from an FBI agent and now an inmate. How similar could they be?

"Freedom is knowing where you've come from and realizing you've been granted an escape from all the ugliness. In my case, God looked at me, saw all of the bad I've done, and said he'd take my punishment. He took all of it, so I could be free from the guilt and shame and embarrassment of everything I'd done. I am free."

Similar to her Papá's words. Completely opposite from Jeremy's. All Selena knew is God seemed pretty distant to her, like he was watching from the sidelines. She was the active player in the game of life. Jolie said God had plans for her specifically, but why? Why would God care about her, specifically? Especially when there were so many people out there. And this freedom thing? She'd never been an anxious person or a worrier. She made decisions based on what she thought would be best for her and let everyone else worry about their own things. Not much need for a God in her life.

"And yet, you're here," She didn't want to kill his dramatic speech, but realistically, he wasn't physically free.

"I also believe in consequences and responses to my actions." Brandon looked out the window. "I am free in here." Brandon tapped his chest. "Regardless of my surroundings, I'm free emotionally and spiritually."

"And the four people you killed? How free are they?"

Brandon turned to look at her. Seconds passed. Only after a knock on the interior door did either of them look away.

Jeremy stood at the door leading into the administration building. Surprised, Selena unlocked the door and stepped out of his way. He plunked into the seat across from her desk.

"Okay…" both Brandon and Selena said at the same time. Brandon pulled his institutional gray ball hat out of his back pocket and pushed it farther down on his face. Jeremy looked from one to the other.

"You can leave." Selena dismissed Brandon, feeling Jeremy's eyes upon her. "If I need you, I'll call down to the housing unit." She'd follow up on their conversation later.

Jeremy swung his feet up on her desk after Brandon left. "What was that all about? You could cut the tension in half."

"It was nothing. I was confronting him about these gang leaders, and he got touchy."

"I know he's an inmate, but who is he in here?" Jeremy slouched lower in the chair.

"Just Sam's clerk. He runs for me when I need him." A thought flittered past her mind before she could stop it. She needed him? The inmate clerk? Brandon? Only to run, only to run. Selena stepped closer to Jeremy. Dark circles under his eyes and more than a 5 o'clock shadow grew on his face.

"Ahh…Sam. Your friend. I'm sorry. I'm a little upside down today. It's been a rough one." Jeremy stretched out over the desk and caught her hand. "Really, I'm sorry."

"You look like you haven't slept at all." Selena enjoyed the warmth of his hand but warily glanced at the window. Anyone walking by could see them holding hands over the table. Selena pulled her hand away and brushed imaginary dust off her desk.

"My sister's not doing well. Did I tell you she has cancer?"

Selena shook her head. How can he be irritating and endearing all at the same time?

"She's been battling for about a year now. I keep thinking she's going to pull out of it, and then she takes a turn for the worse." Jeremy laid his head down on the desk. "I know there's nothing I can do, but I just keep thinking I should be doing something."

Selena sat quietly, wondering what to say. Maybe listening was what he wanted. Reaching out her hand, she softly brushed cinnamon brown curls on his neck.

"Where is she? Somewhere far away?" Selena asked.

"In Texas, not too far. Around the Dallas area so she can be close to the best medical facility."

She jumped as the door to her office flew open. DeNickey stood, leering at them.

13

"Well, if it ain't the two love birds."

Selena glared at him.

"What? Did I interrupt something?" A devilish smile played across DeNickey's face.

"No." Jeremy leaned back in the chair, feet once again on her desk. All vulnerability gone; the professional FBI agent was back.

"Really. Well, stop by my office before you leave and we'll talk." DeNickey pointed at Jeremy and sauntered out the door.

"What could he possibly want?" Jeremy tilted his head, resting it on the back of the chair.

"What *does* he want?" Selena put her elbows on the desk, chin in her hands.

"It's all a job. He has things I need; I have things he needs."

"Hmmm…" Selena wondered what Jeremy could need from DeNickey. It was obvious DeNickey could work a career move by using an FBI agent like he did everyone else. Selena, herself, was awed by the reality of hanging out with someone in the FBI. Imagine the connections DeNickey thought Jeremy could work for him.

"Well, I need to go see what he wants. Oh, I brought you this." Jeremy pulled out a chocolate candy bar. "To hold you over until tonight."

Selena slid the chocolate into a desk drawer. "What's tonight?"

"I thought, maybe, if you were free, we could go to dinner. I can tell you more about my sister. Without DeNickey barging in on us."

"Are you asking me out? Like a date?"

"Uh, yes. Like a date." Jeremy stood.

"Ask."

He shook his head. "You are so bull-headed. Do you want to go out or not?"

Selena crossed her arms. "You're going to have to do better."

"Shall I get on bended knee?"

"Shut up. 8 o'clock, my house." Selena scribbled down the address.

"It's a date." Jeremy winked at her.

Her feelings were always upside down with Jeremy. One minute she was attracted to his confidence and power, the next minute she wanted to drop-kick him. And if she were honest, she liked the sparring between them.

"Hey, Maldanado. You in there?" Selena jumped when she heard the intercom on her phone shout. She had to remember the intercom worked both ways. Not only could the Orientation Office call her on the intercom, but they could also listen to what was being said in her office.

"Yeah, I'm here. Did you need something?"

"We've got a bunch of inmates coming in Receiving from one of the other prisons. We could use your help if you're free."

"Be there in a few."

Selena walked down the short hallway and entered Receiving just as an officer was putting an inmate in handcuffs.

"You're real bright." The officer sneered as he told him to stand on the painted line on the floor. The inmate shuffled his feet over to the line.

"What happened?"

"He had dope on him. Tried to conceal it in his sock. What an idiot."

"He came in like that? Think the sending prison knew it? Setting us up?"

"I don't know. I'll take him down to the Hole in a minute."

"This all the stuff you picked off the inmates in the bunch?" Selena took a pen and rifled through the things on the table. No way was she touching them with bare hands. Forks, later fashioned into shanks, nude pictures, gum, and various other contraband littered the table.

As the officers continued to strip search the newly arrived inmates, Selena issued the normal prison gear, blanket, pillow, two sets of institutional clothing and the standard boots.

Looking up as the last inmate was booked, she picked up the paperwork from the transferred inmates. "Want me to take these files to Classification?"

"Great. Thanks for the help." A lieutenant led the pack out of Receiving and down onto the yard.

~

Hours later, Selena capped her pen and went in

search of a Diet Coke. She could walk down to Sam as he had an endless supply, but the machine in the officer's lounge was closer. Locking up the files on her desk, Selena walked past DeNickey's closed door and through the hall. Stopping midway, she lifted her nose in the air. Is that pot? She couldn't possibly be smelling marijuana. Selena raised her eyebrows. From what she could tell, the smell was coming from outside the Orientation room. The guards should have turned in the confiscated pot to the investigator by now.

Selena pulled the door open to the outer gate as one of the Orientation officers put the rolled cigarette up to his lips. "What are you doing? Are you crazy?"

Continuing to look at her through half-slit eyes, the officer shrugged. The other guard stood, feet squared, watching smoke curl around his head.

"The investigator told us to keep it. He said we needed a reward."

"The pot we got off the Receiving inmate? You've got to be out of your mind." Selena looked at both of them again. Neither seemed concerned. Could they really have the investigator's consent?

Stomping down the hall to DeNickey's office, Selena saw the light on and threw open his door without knocking.

"Excuse me?" DeNickey had his music on, a mix of creepy ballads.

"We took pot off a kid coming in from Receiving this afternoon. Did they give it to you?" she demanded.

"Yeah, and I gave it back to them."

"What? What is wrong with you people?"

"Oh, cool off. It was only tea."

"Only tea? Sure smelled like pot to me."

"And you would know what pot smells like how?" DeNickey grinned as he ran a file under his nails, scooping the dirt onto the floor.

Selena grimaced. No telling how much fingernail crud she'd walked through when she came through the door.

"Really, it's just tea. Inmates figured out how to roll tea bags and smoke them, gives only a minor buzz, but it's better than nothing."

"That was not tea." She suspected the guards had known what DeNickey was saying and were probably laughing at her now.

"Yes, it was. I tested it. There's a company makes tea smelling like marijuana but without any illegal ingredients. Look it up. Or trust me." He smiled at her again. Selena's spine shivered, looking at his face and the humor at her expense.

"Fine." Selena backed out of the door and returned to her desk, Coke-less and humiliated. The best thing about the day was it would be over soon, and she'd be out with Jeremy for the evening.

14

Eight p.m. sharp brought Jeremy on her doorstep wearing a casual button-down shirt and khaki slacks. A bouquet of daisies complemented his outfit.

"Thank you. How did you know I like daisies?"

"Didn't put you as a roses-type of girl." Jeremy stepped in as she went to the kitchen for a vase.

"Don't know what that means, but I'll take it."

Jeremy bent down to scratch the ear of her Newfoundland puppy, who eagerly rolled to her back, encouraging Jeremy to rub her tummy. "Who might you be?"

"Patches. I just got her a couple of weeks ago. Isn't she cute?" Selena said from the doorway. The dog followed her into the kitchen and slid to a stop at her feet. "She always thinks it's dinner time."

"I like her. She'll make a good watch dog." Jeremy picked up her coat off the back of the couch and held it out for Selena to put her arms through, causing her heart to flutter.

Out in his Lexus SUV, Jeremy turned on a local country station on the radio and opened the sunroof. Part way to the restaurant, he reached over for

Selena's hand. Again, her heart shook. She examined his fingertips with their small white crescent moon shapes in the center. They were clean with no trace of nail crud. No rings graced his fingers either, they were simply long and slender and looked perfect, intertwined with hers. Despite the day she'd had, Selena felt herself beginning to relax as she tilted her head back to catch the slight breeze from the open sunroof.

Their conversation ranged from her prison stories to his FBI career, each sharing more and more of their lives. Twice she found herself checking her breathing, filling her lungs, and forcing herself to believe she really was out with a gorgeous FBI agent.

"Your sister is younger than you? By how much?" Seated in a quiet place in the restaurant, Selena took a bite of salad. The restaurant, known for its legendary steaks, was heavy with cowboy charm, leather seating areas, and low lighting.

"She's six years younger. I'm the big brother who can do no wrong." Jeremy laughed and then said in a serious tone, "I can't do any right in this situation, though. She's probably not going to be here long and there isn't a thing I can do about it. If I could take it on myself, or pay someone to take it away, or I don't know…it's just tough."

Selena reached out her hand to him. She was falling for Jeremy. Jeremy was kind, thoughtful, caring, strong, and good-looking, why shouldn't she fall for him?

Jeremy squeezed her hand, running his thumb over hers. Warmth crept between them.

"Did you know my sister calls me Germy?" He

smiled a boyish grin.

"Germy? I like it." Selena smiled back.

"My father, on the other hand, calls me Jeremiah. He believes I should follow in his wake and be a lawyer, a Capitol Hill type."

"Wow. He doesn't like you being FBI?"

"He doesn't think it's much more than law enforcement. To be honest, he's probably right; it's just specialized police work."

"But a Special Agent isn't anything to sneeze at."

Jeremy gave an appreciative glance that warmed her all the way to her toes. He might not be high-powered enough for his father, but he was way up there in Selena's mind.

Selena told Jeremy about the pot they found and catching the Orientation guards smoking it.

"The worst part is DeNickey gave it to them as a reward for a job well done."

"He gave it to them?"

"Yes. What they didn't tell me was it wasn't really pot…it's a kind of tea you can smoke, and it smells like pot. Can you believe that? I'm pretty sure what I saw was pot. They said it was what they got off the Receiving inmate, but I'm finding it hard to believe DeNickey would give them real pot or that the officers would smoke it on prison grounds."

"Tea that smells like pot? I've heard of guys smoking tea bags but not ones smelling like pot. Are you sure?"

"Well, that's what DeNickey said. I wouldn't be so mad if I'd known it before I jumped down those guards' throats. It just looked like it was set up to make me look stupid. And it did. I'm pretty sure it wasn't the same pot I saw found on the inmate."

"Hey, I wouldn't get too sideways about it. DeNickey's a jerk."

"What did he want from you?" Selena stuck her fork in a perfectly cooked piece of steak.

"Want? Political stuff. Hey, how's your dinner?"

Selena studied him, noticing his tone. She was right, DeNickey treated everyone the same.

The remaining dinner was consumed with light talk as Selena enjoyed her dinner. Was it possible to be this lucky? A good looking, FBI agent as her dinner date. Was he too good to be true?

~

Brandon lay on his bunk, fingers interlaced behind his head. Tonight had been a bust, a waste of time. He'd attended the church meeting held every Wednesday night in the little room off the library, but the message just depressed him. The volunteer chaplain had spoken a lot about a little and none of it had grabbed Brandon's attention.

What had caught his eye were the groups of men drawn to the church service. Maldanado was right. Many were there only to socialize and meet with others in their group without causing suspicion among the guards. Bandanas hanging from left or right pockets, shoelaces double knotted, and visible tattoos separated the gang banger sects. Brandon could only see one or two men who looked as if they were actually attending for the sake of the message. The poor civilian who had been picked from his church to lead the prison ministry tried in vain to capture their attention by raising his voice to "fire and brimstone" levels. Brandon never understood those types of preachers. The man preached like religion was a punishment, something hot and unyielding. He knew his own religious experience had been nothing like that. It was more like a soothing, warm blanket covering all of the ugly, scratchy places in his life. God's mercy and grace had left him with a peace transcending his present circumstances. Suzie was right. He wasn't like the others here. He knew the love of a Savior who had swooped him out of quicksand and dusted him off. He could taste true freedom. Most of these guys had never experienced that depth of love. Maldanado had been right in another way, too. Christianity, to most of those sitting around him in the chapel, was only discussed at parole hearing time.

Brandon had walked back to his cell, unfulfilled. He had needed something more to sooth his agitation, something deeper than a physical release. He had hoped listening to the chaplain would help, but it didn't ease the restlessness.

The only thing that resonated with him was the scripture read in such a loud voice it belied the entire tone of what Brandon actually read. He'd looked it up when he got into his cell. Isaiah 61:1. He knew all about Jesus coming for the broken-hearted and trading mourning for gladness, but the part about the darkness being released for the prisoners jumped at him. There was a day coming when eyes would be opened to the injustice that hid in the darkness. He prayed Maldanado was on the right side of that promise.

15

Selena returned to her office the next day to find a bouquet of roses sitting in the middle of her desk. The yellow roses, completely opened, with tufts of baby's breath scattered between, comprised the huge arrangement.

"What is this?" Selena said out loud. Jeremy's flowers were still at home on her counter, and she'd been impressed with his choice of daisies. Roses were overwhelming and gaudy and made her head hurt.

"What?" Selena picked up the phone on the third ring.

Opening the card, she read, *Wanted you to know you are appreciated.* Ron DeNickey. Ewww… Selena picked up the bundle, dripping water on her desk calendar, and threw them upside down in the trash. Selena rolled her eyes when she thought of who might have seen him bring them in. Ewww…Ewww… EWWWW.

"Wow. Good morning to you, too." Sam said on the other end.

"Sorry." Selena slumped down into her chair. "DeNickey sent me flowers."

"Wow again. Be careful. Not a good sign."

"I know. I tossed them. I wanted to pull every single one of the petals off just like I'd like to do to his eyes, his ears, every slimy piece of hair."

"Okay, well, want to come help me? I'm locking two guys up for threatening letters and a tattoo gun floating somewhere in Housing Unit 3." Sam offered a way out of the stifling, rose-scented office.

"Absolutely. Be there in a minute." Selena turned to find DeNickey standing in her doorway.

"A thank you would have sufficed." DeNickey stated, pointing at the flowers in the trash.

"They had worms." Selena scooped up her briefcase and stalked out the door to the yard. Heat infused her face. That would probably cost her somewhere down the road.

Avoiding his advances was one thing; blatantly shutting him down was another. As Selena entered the bubble area and checked in, she noticed the e-squad doing cell searches in one of the wings. Bedding was flung from the upper walkway. It looked like a tornado had hit.

"Who's running the camera down there?"

"Sterlen." The guard pointed at another officer, capturing all of the activity on film.

"As long as it isn't me." Selena capped the pen and headed out the bubble door.

"Sam." Selena yelled from the bottom of the steps. "SAM."

Sam's blond crewcut peeked out a cell door. She could hear inmates cussing on the lower level and suspected Sam was getting the verbal onslaught upstairs.

"Come on up. Bring your gloves." Sam yelled at her over the din.

Reaching the doorway, she ignored the glare of the inmate in handcuffs outside the cell, his room apparently. Selena was narrowly missed by flying pornography.

"Ick." Selena kicked it over the side of the railing to the other trash below.

The cuffed inmate started to say something vulgar to her but was brought up short by the officer next to him.

"These guys think it's cute to have their girlfriends pose for them and send in their pictures," Sam paused in his search. "What they forget is, who's taking the picture of their naked girlfriend? Stupid."

"You thought I was grumpy." Selena pulled on gloves. "Still looking for the tatt gun?"

"Yes, and everything else. Word is there's a couple of shanks floating around, too." Sam opened a bottle of shampoo and swished the contents around.

Several cells later, Selena carefully dumped a boot over the bed. Clunking to the floor was a contraption of metal, a 9 Volt battery, guitar wire, and a couple of dominoes.

"Ay, yi, yi. Look at this."

"And there she is. Beginning of a tattoo gun, if you ask me. The only thing they're missing is the pen."

Selena turned the dominoes over in her hand. "Why anyone would want to melt these and insert it under their skin is a mystery to me."

"I know. One of the other housing units found a

spot in the shower where they'd been burning them down." Sam reached for the dominoes. Sliding everything back into the boot, he stepped outside the cell and waved it in the inmate's face. Selena could hear Sam taunting him about his "lost" possession.

"Hey, I'm going to the next cell. Are you about done here?" Selena tossed her gloves over the side of the walk and pulled her hair back into a ponytail with a rubber band.

"Okay. Put your gloves back on."

After having the next cell's inmates handcuffed and positioned outside the room, Selena stopped to survey the contents. In training, the staff had been taught to look at everything first and then work from one side of the room to the other in a systematic pattern. The room stunk as most of the cells did, smelling of urine and unwashed bodies.

Besides the bathroom fixtures, the bunk beds were the only piece of furniture. Cabinets without locking capabilities held the incarcerated man's toiletries and clothing.

Starting on one side of the room, Selena leafed through paperback books left on the upper bunk.

Tossing the thin, gray sheet to the floor, Selena pulled off the mattress cover and swung the mattress down to the ground. After checking every seam for tears or rips, places to stash contraband, she laid it up against the end of the bed. With her flashlight, she ran the small orb of light around the metal frame.

When nothing presented itself on the top bunk, she moved to the lower bunk. Same thing, strip the sheet, toss the mattress pad, and turn it over and around. Running her flashlight around each corner,

Selena spotted a scratch on the metal underneath the top bunk. Sitting on the metal frame, she leaned under the bunk to see what was written.

In disbelief, she took a breath, and then leaned closer.

Maldanado.

Her name, scratched right into the metal. Hitting her head on the upper bunk, she swung her feet around in front of her. Selena felt her stomach tighten. The scratches were just that, scratches. But it was clearly her name.

Selena jumped up, nearly hitting her head on the bunk again. Standing outside the door was the first person she would talk to.

"So, Inmate…Lee," Selena started in a low voice, reading the name on his clothing. "How long have you been in this cell?"

"Just a day, ma'am." The chunky man in handcuffs looked at the floor.

"Are you top bunk or lower bunk?"

"Top."

"Where's your cellmate?" Growing frustrated, her palms began to sweat.

"At court."

"And how long has he been there?"

"I don't know."

"I'm sure you saw what's written on the bunk." Selena's voice went up a notch, enough to cause Sam to come out of the cell he was searching.

"Hey, what's wrong?" Sam stepped up, glancing between Selena and the inmate.

The man was silent.

Blowing out a breath, Selena led Sam into the

room and pointed out the writing in the metal.

"Wow. Could mean a lot of different things." Sam studied the scratches. "Maybe you have an admirer."

"Of all the lame brain…" Selena punched Sam in the arm, hard.

"Owww. Jeez, I was kidding."

"Like having my name written on the bottom of a bunk is funny?"

"I guess you haven't seen it in the men's staff bathroom yet?"

"You have got to be kidding." Selena moved, inches from Sam's laughing face.

"Come on. There's nothing to this. What? They wrote it on the bunk and then what?"

"It could mean a lot of things. Maybe I ticked someone off, and I'm a target." The nausea built in her throat again.

"Wait a minute. You're blowing this out of proportion. You are single, female, good-looking I might add, smart, work for the Investigator, and you might be a target? Honey, you are a target and always will be. Unless you go and get ugly or something. Naw, that wouldn't even work."

Selena looked at the floor, heat building in her ears and blotching her chest and neck.

"Look, I'll have it painted over and no one will know any more about it." Sam reached out and touched her arm.

Jerking away from him, Selena stomped past.

~

"Dude, what's up with her?" the bubble officer asked Sam as he logged in the cell searches.

"I don't know. Bad day, I guess."

"Bad week, more like. She's been acting crazy ever since she caught those Receiving officers smoking dope outside."

"Doing what?" Sam turned his full attention to the young officer. The E-squad remained in the housing unit, systematically searching the remaining cells. The floors in the house were barely visible with mattresses and sheets and contraband strewn all over.

"It turned out to be a kind of tea that smells like grass, and I guess, she went off on them. The more they talked, the hotter she got 'cause I guess the Investigator gave it to them as a joke."

"Hadn't heard yet. Well, that'd stir the bees under my bonnet, too."

Sam walked back to his office. He knew the relationship between Selena and the Investigator was already inappropriate, but it looked like he'd set her up, made her the brunt of his joke. And Sam knew Selena wouldn't sit down for that. But it would be a long road to travel if she filed harassment charges against the investigator. With her run-in with the tea-smoking guards, plus the incident today, Sam still felt as if there was more bothering Selena that she wasn't sharing. And if it was something she wasn't telling Sam, then it probably had to do with Jeremy. Maybe.

Maybe he should just send her a Diet Coke and move on to the growing mountain of contraband the E-squad was leaving on his desk.

16

"Anything strange in that cell you want to tell me about?" Selena leaned over the scarred interview table. She had a list of the inmates who'd been assigned to the cell, and she intended to talk to every one of them. Selena had to find out if this was just an admirer like Sam insisted. Her gut told her it was more.

"Nope. Saw your name on the bunk, but I didn't write it." The tall, black inmate sucked his teeth and wiped his hands on his pants as he waited for her questions.

"How do I know that?" Selena glared at him.

"Officer, I'm only here to do my time. I'm here on shock probation, and I don't intend to do anything to get me more time. Ain't no way."

"Alright, he can go back to his cell." Selena told the transporting officer. She would have sensed his fear, but all she noticed was his nervousness about being in the investigation room.

Checking her list, she marked off the most recent inmate and scrolled further down. One was still at court and hadn't been in the cell for months. Two were no longer incarcerated at this prison, and the fourth didn't seem to have any animosity toward her. Five remaining.

Next up on her list was an African American with vivid green eyes. In the hole for fighting with another inmate over basketball time, he seemed unlikely to be the culprit as he was only in the cell for a short period of time. Her viewpoint changed, though, as he walked in with a smirk on his face. Before he reached the door, she noticed Brandon standing off to the side, holding the familiar thick envelope in his hand. Grateful for Sam's thoughtfulness again, she accepted the envelope carrying Diet Coke and watched as the inmate sat down across the table from her.

After checking his name against her files, Selena asked the mundane questions first: What's your charge? Why were you in the hole? Who's your cellmate right now? As her questions became more specific, the inmate began to rock back and forth in his wooden chair.

Irritated by his smugness, Selena finally asked, "What is your deal?"

"Got something for you."

Selena stood. Usually, she wasn't apprehensive about being alone in a room with an inmate without a weapon of any sort, but his cockiness was creating an uncharacteristic wariness. Her radar was on high alert.

"It's in my pocket. Can I get it?"

"What is it?"

"Just a piece of paper." The inmate smiled at her revealing a gold tooth on the side of his mouth.

"Better be or you'll never get out of the hole."

"It is, I promise." Slowly, the African American reached his handcuffed arm around to his side pocket and pulled out a small triangle of paper. Unfolding it so she could see the writing, he held it in front of him, unwilling to hand it to her.

Selena stared at the little piece of paper. Her full name neatly written in block letters.

SELENA GRACE MALDANADO

Glancing at the inmate, Selena saw a glimmer of greed mixed with outright pleasure. Selena continued to stare at him. The inmate grinned at her. Putting her hand out, she reached out to take the paper, noticing her fingers were shaking slightly.

"Naw, I don't think so." The inmate casually put it in his mouth and chewed it like an unimportant piece of paper.

Selena watched, wishing she did have a weapon, one big enough to knock it back out of his mouth. The inmate casually spit the now wet and unrecognizable wad out on the table.

"Am I supposed to care about my name on a piece of paper?"

"I was told you would." He sucked his teeth again.

"Why? Why would I have any desire to care about you writing my name on a bunk or a piece of paper or a wall?" Selena stood and leaned against the wall.

"A wall? I ain't never seen it on a wall. Or a bunk." The inmate shook his head.

"Forget it. Why did you want me to see it?"

"I was told the investigator could get me whatever I wanted. When I wanted something, I just had to show the name."

Selena could hear sounds outside the room, guards talking, phones ringing, but time stood still in the interview room. She sat back down in the chair across from him and tried to make sense of what he'd said.

Whatever they wanted? She swallowed the nausea rising in her throat.

"Aw, come on, man. You know what's I'm talking about. Blow. Weed. Wo-men. Whatever." The inmate rocked back in his chair.

"And my name is what you are supposed to show? To who?" Selena put her hands on the table and leaned into the inmate's space. Is this a joke? Another one of DeNickey's sad ways to set her up? What if the inmate was telling the truth? Did all of the inmates know about this?

"Why yours, pretty lady. Anything I want." He grinned, not answering the second question.

"Get out. Now." Selena pushed the door open. "NOW. He's done."

Slowly, the inmate followed the guard out into the wing. "I'll be in touch."

Selena muttered under her breath and resisted the urge to slam the door behind him. Her name was out there as the supplier of contraband, drugs, hooch, to the general population? It didn't make sense. She'd never had one inappropriate interaction with an inmate. Never. Never even questioned. The stupid inmate had to be yanking her chain, baiting her. There had never, and would never, be a reason to believe she was corrupt in her dealings with anyone. Unless DeNickey was setting her up.

~

Brandon watched as the last inmate left the interview office. He'd heard rumors on the yard, and if Maldanado was dirty like they were saying, well, let the pieces fall where they may. Brandon kicked a cigarette butt on the ground. Life was bound to get a little harder before it got easier. He shook his head. He was hoping she wasn't involved with anything he was investigating, but info coming his way told a different story. Just when he was beginning to doubt her involvement, all arrows pointed back to her. Maybe he wanted to believe differently. When this job was done and he was out, he wanted to…   No sense in that thinking. It wouldn't matter if he were the one to bring all them to justice.

~

A late lunch outside the prison walls didn't improve Selena's thoughts as she rushed past Sam signing out his radio at the front airlock. Between finding her name scrawled on the bunk to the idiot inmate who thought she was a connection for him, Selena was stretched tight. She chewed on her cuticle until it bled.

"Hey. What's up?" Sam jogged after her. He stopped as she entered the women's restroom.

Selena paused before the mirror and took two deep breaths. She was mad, really mad. There was too much drama, and somehow, she'd landed in the thick of it. Washing her hands at the faucet, she dampened a towel and ran it over her neck, careful not to drip on her dress clothes.

Ay, yi, yi. She had to get out of here for a while. Beyond an hour lunch break.

Selena felt the tension slide up her spine and flower out over her shoulders. Rolling her head around on her neck, Selena attempted to release some of it. Wishing she smoked, Selena gazed at the frown lines on her face. There'd probably be more wrinkles if she smoked. Selena sighed. Chocolate and her remaining pop would have to do for today.

Selena left the restroom only to find Sam still in the hallway waiting on her.

"What is wrong with you? Bad hair day?"

Selena shot him an ugly look. "I'm fine." Before he could ask any more questions, she signed for her radio and headed down to her office. Somehow, she had to find out why her name came up in this mess. Maybe it wasn't a mess at all. Maybe it was an inmate being an inmate, and Sam was right about the admirer. Unfortunately, the bile caught in her throat, and the rolling in her gut said something different.

17

Selena snaked a hand out from under the warm blanket and hit the snooze button. Her body ached and griped about the movement. She must have picked up a bug somewhere. Or the stress was doing a number on her body. Despite her pounding head, she got out of bed and called in sick. DeNickey didn't answer his phone so she left a message informing him of her sick day. DeNickey's smart remarks were the last thing she wanted today; she was happy to talk to his machine. A bottle of water and two aspirins downed, Selena took her favorite blanket and a pillow to the couch and drifted back to sleep.

Several hours later, a light tapping on her front door brought Selena up through the murky waters of a dream. She was being chased by an alien which looked un-surprisingly like DeNickey. It was only a dream. Only a dream. Relieved, she tried to shake off the twinges of fear and bring reality back into focus. She muttered to herself as she peeked through the eyehole.

Jeremy stood on the other side, shifting his weight from foot to foot.

Patting her hair, but knowing it was a disaster with no time for a fix, Selena opened the door.

"Wow, you don't look good," Jeremy placed a paper bag on the floor and cupped her cheeks in his hands. "You're really flushed." Gently, placing his lips on her forehead, he stated, "but not running a fever. Mom always did that."

~

Stepping back out of the doorway, Selena invited him in as he gathered his bag. Reluctantly. She'd change when he saw what he had in the bag. She was beautiful, even sick and in clothes that looked like they'd been slept in.

"How'd you know I was home?" Selena asked, peeking into the bag.

"DeNickey. He said you left a message. I figured I'd bring over something."

"How noble of you." Selena wiped her nose with a Kleenex.

"Not too sick to feud with me, I see. Can't even give a little credit to the handsome guy who brings you food?"

"Hmpf."

Jeremy smiled as she dug into the bag. She fascinated him from the time she had entered his classroom and the big things about her, like her fiery attitude and her sassy mouth, had seriously attracted him. Constantly baiting her and pushing her buttons was fun, the tension between them was palatable. And who could miss her silky hair and perfectly contoured figure? No one.

Watching her pull egg drop soup and chocolate ice cream bars from the bag, Jeremy concentrated on the woman in front of him.

~

Selena grinned as she unpacked his sack of goodies. Kleenex and three kinds of medicine followed the soup and frozen treats. Despite the heat outside, Selena thought the warmth of soup flowing down her raw throat sounded heavenly.

"Why all the medicine, Germy?" Selena laughed as Jeremy winced at the nickname.

"Well, DeNickey said you were sick, so I brought medicine for a cold," he held up a clear bottle filled with purple liquid, "medicine for allergies, and in case it was more of the female variety…well, the bottle says it covers all that."

Selena smirked at his discomfort. "You brought me medicine just in case I was PMSing? Wow, aren't you the good guy?"

Jeremy shrugged again and turned his back to her, ears red.

"I really think it's drainage from allergies. I've had them since I was a kid," Selena blew her nose. "But the soup is perfect."

A comfortable silence enveloped them as they poured the fragrant liquid into bowls and settled on the couch.

"I think I'm going to take tomorrow off, too," Selena sipped the warm soup. "Yesterday was such a crappy day. Do you know I found my name written on a bunk and when I questioned one inmate, he insinuated word on the yard was the investigator could get him anything he wanted? I know there are dirty guards, but I'm not one of them." Selena used her napkin to wipe her nose. "I was supposed to go to my father's this weekend. I believe I'll leave a day earlier. DeNickey won't miss me."

"Right. He was bemoaning your absence today." Jeremy laid a sock-clad foot up on the coffee table. In khaki shorts and a faded T-shirt, Jeremy looked even more alluring than when he wore his more professional work clothes. His casualness softened his edges. "Does he know about all this? What you just told me?"

"No." With a twinge of guilt, Selena rethought her earlier decision to stay out another day. Maybe she should go in. If anything came up at the prison while she was away, she knew DeNickey would hand off the investigating, her job, to the cutest guard on shift. He'd done it to her before.

"Where does your father live again?" Jeremy brought her out of her thoughts.

Selena cocked her head to the side. "He's on a cattle ranch in Texas. Well, it's more than a cattle ranch; it's become more like a little town. They now have a boardinghouse, a mail station, a cantina, even a small campground."

"Why so many things?"

A conversation without a battle? Good. Selena laid her head back on the couch.

"It used to be a standard ranch with a bunkhouse," Selena yawned. "Then my father and the man who owns the ranch started hosting several big events like rodeos, cowboy action shooting, youth camps, western vacation campouts. It's a pretty big operation now."

"Do I get to go with you?" Jeremy tugged a loose curl on her shoulder.

Selena turned her head to look at him. Dark brown eyes met hers. Not only was he touching her hair, again, but he wanted to go to the ranch with her?

"Uh, no."

"You know what? We started this whole thing wrong. Let's pretend." Jeremy pulled her into the crook of his shoulder. He tucked her in tighter as Selena started to pull away. "Nope, stay put."

"Pretend what?"

"Pretend this is fun. That we might actually enjoy hanging out together."

Jeremy smoothed curls away from her face, over his shoulder.

"Why are we doing this again?"

"Just stay here for two minutes and then if you don't want to, then you can move."

"What makes you think I'm going to be compliant?" Battling was safer. The heat where their bodies touched was nearly her undoing. He was warm and comforting and nice…and smelled great.

"Can you please stop your lips from moving for a moment?"

Selena stayed still. Forcing breaths from her lips, she counted. . . 58 . . . 59 . . .60 . .1 . . .2 . . . Selena slowly closed her eyes and drifted off. She was vaguely aware Jeremy was snoring quietly, arm still wrapped around her.

~

Jeremy opened his eyes to tingling sensations running up and down his arm. Turning his head, he could see Selena, with her face uplifted to his, snuggled in his embrace. Mouth slightly open, she breathed shallowly, and her long eyelashes fluttered in sleep. She was definitely beautiful. Jeremy closed his eyes. She was not going to be happy when she found out what DeNickey was doing. Jeremy didn't like it any better, but he had yet to find a way out. It would make an end to this, before it ever really got started.

~

"Dios mio. Did we fall asleep?" Selena bucked off the couch.

"Kinda. Just for a bit." Jeremy mused.

Selena pushed hair off her face. Late afternoon. They'd slept more than an hour, curled on the couch together.

"Do you feel better?" Jeremy stood, stretching.

"Yeah, but you'd better go." How embarrassing. She scrambled to find an emotion to settle on. Comfy? Stupid? Excited? Foolish?

"Again, do I get to come with you this weekend?" Hand on the door, he looked at her expectantly.

"No. And again, No." Selena met him at the door.

"Okay." Jeremy frowned at her. "Well, think about this while you're gone. . . maybe those inmates you were talking about, the ones who are putting your name on the 'dirty cop list'? You aren't the only investigator in the prison. Maybe they got the wrong investigator." With a final look at her, he shut the door behind him.

Wait. . . what? She and DeNickey were the only investigators right now. Was he suggesting DeNickey was dirty?

Yanking the door back open, Selena watched

Jeremy get in his SUV and drive off. She should have stopped him; asked him what he knew, why he would say he believed the inmate, believed the Investigator's office was the source of the contraband on the yard? Jeremy and DeNickey were involved with each other, did he know more than he'd indicated? Could Jeremy be involved? No, Jeremy was FBI, even though corruption was everywhere, she couldn't imagine Jeremy hooking up with someone like DeNickey.

Nauseated, Selena closed the door and slid to the bottom.

18

DeNickey stepped into the smoky room, taking in the clusters of people sitting at the bar or around tables. The music was deafening.

How revolting, He chose a stool next to a lady with empty seats around her. He didn't mind rock music, although not at ear-piercing levels. The resounding bass and drumbeat spoke to the darker, guttural side of nature. However, the singer was butchering the lyrics. DeNickey shook his head.

"A little loud, ain't it?" The lady leaned over to him, blowing smoke in his direction.

He resisted the urge to slap her. Instead, he smiled, squinting his eyes in response to the face full of smoke. Holding his breath until the plumes had passed, he waited, digesting every detail of the not-so-young woman in front of him. Dark roots exposed her failed attempt to look younger. Her gauzy white top and black lace bra underneath raised the intensity of his gaze. She seemed to shrink under his ogling, but wasn't that what she wanted? Women, they were so transparent. He could see the need in her eyes.

"Yes, it is. Are you waiting for someone?" DeNickey broke eye contact and returned to looking around the room and the rest of the body sitting next to him. She repulsed him. How easily she could be taken. His appetite to do what he wanted, with who he wanted, when he wanted was growing.

The woman chortled and looked at her watch. "Yeah, for about another ten years."

"Ah." DeNickey had known when he approached her she was one of them. "Them" as in an inmate's girlfriend or wife; the kind that moved to where their loved one was to visit regularly.

DeNickey didn't care why they were here. They were simply opportunities for him. Opportunities to fill his need for domination, or an information provider, or even at best, a connection to the world he had carefully concealed for years.

DeNickey half-listened as the woman excused herself to the restroom. She tiptoed on tall stiletto heels, banging into tables and patrons on her way.

The bartender, with his balding head and short thin ponytail, reminded him of the first time he got a taste for that world. An old inmate had requested a favor, a look-the-other-way kind which opened the door for the power DeNickey sought. And the payment for the favor? Connections to drug suppliers, money and opportunities extending through the prison, out the front gates and into the dark underworld.

"I didn't catch your name." The woman returned.

"Does it matter?"

~

Jeremy slid into the haze in the bar and spotted him immediately, sitting with his hand on a sleazy woman's knee. He'd left Selena's place to come to this?

"I'm here." Jeremy leaned across the woman and picked up DeNickey's beer. "I'll have one of these." He hollered to the barkeep. DeNickey's annoyed face amused him. "Scram." Jeremy whispered in the woman's ear. She hastily picked up her drink, eyed both of the men, and stumbled to a far table.

"Now see here. She was just shy of one drink too many. You ruined it." DeNickey pulled his beer back in front of him.

"Sorry. She's not your type anyway. Well, maybe she is. Fifty-something, drunk, and waiting for her beloved, innocent boyfriend to get out of jail. Yeah, that fits you."

"What do you want?" DeNickey growled.

"Just to talk. I'm not thinking our little deal is going quite the way it should." Jeremy said, swirling his drink.

DeNickey looked over his shoulder into the darker parts of the bar.

"Don't worry. Only sleazebags hang out here."

Jeremy double-checked too. He couldn't afford to be seen with DeNickey outside the prison. Of course, looking around, this was as much a part of the correctional world as actually being inside.

"Why do you think our deal isn't going the way you want it to?"

"Well, Selena said there was pot in Receiving confiscated, but I know for a fact it wasn't my stuff."

"Oh, you mean, the tea?" DeNickey chortled. "That was fun. She was definitely fired up."

"No, the real stuff. She said it wasn't tea." Jeremy resisted the urge to punch him in the face. "Regardless, I still want out. I'm done."

"I remember when you first came to me. A snot-nosed, wanna-be gang banger riding motorcycles with the big dogs."

"First of all, I didn't come to you. You were in my conference workshop, and you approached me."

"You were pretty desperate to make quick money if I recall."

Jeremy blew out a breath. He'd made the mistake of getting really drunk and spilling his guts to the man about how he wanted to pay off his sick sister's hospital bills. DeNickey had been sympathetic to his plight and offered opportunities. His connections inside the prison versus Jeremy's connections in the undercover world.

"What are you thinking?" Jeremy had asked.

"Know anyone with some dope they want off their hands?"

There it was, out on the table, exactly where Jeremy thought it was going. The man was probably wearing a wire. Just his luck. Jeremy stared at him.

DeNickey stared back. "You think on it. You'd bring it in from wherever, give it to my contact, they'd distribute it, and we'll split the profit. Easy."

"So, I'd be a mule." The thought had depressed him. Trying to raise extra money for his sister, and he was being reduced to a mule. Life was spiraling downward once again.

"A rich one, though." was the reply.

A hefty bank account later, Jeremy agreed the stress level had decreased after paying off many of the bills, but his self-depreciation had deepened.

If his sister had gotten well, he would have dumped DeNickey, moved to Alaska and worked as a hunting guide. If only…

"What's with you and Maldanado, anyway?" DeNickey's voice jolted him back to the smoky bar. Unfortunately, he was still here, still feeling trapped.

"Leave Selena out of it."

"I thought since you were tight now, you'd tell her everything." DeNickey sneered at him. "You telling me she doesn't know your bike is loaded with dope?"

"She doesn't. She doesn't know anything. Except that you're a jerk." Jeremy ran his fingers through his hair, causing the curls to stand away from his head.

"Oh, dear. I've upset you." DeNickey squeaked, feigning concern.

"I want out. I'm done." Jeremy repeated and tossed dollar bills on the bar.

"Not so fast, bad boy. You'll get out when I say, not when you decide. You'll keep doing this until I decide I'm done with you. And if you don't… well, I may have to pay a visit to your pretty, little Selena." DeNickey scoffed at him, standing as well. "She may not be so pretty after I'm done with her."

19

Jeremy sulked to his SUV. DeNickey was an idiot, an idiot that had him in the crosshairs. He had to find a way out, even if it destroyed both of them. Unlocking his door, he didn't notice the meaty fist hit him from the side.

He dodged another blow and swiped at his now, bloody nose. The man swinging at him beat him by fifty pounds which all seemed to be in his right hook. Catching a kick to his thigh, Jeremy stumbled and was rewarded with another fist in his ear.

"Come on, pumpkin. Let's go have a talk." The big man grabbed Jeremy around the neck and drug him to the front of the vehicle.

Spun around to face his attacker, Jeremy looked at the man through blood dripping down his face. He tried to memorize his features. Two gold earrings in his left ear, a spider web tattoo spread over his neck, bulging blue eyes over a shaggy beard.

"The man inside wanted to leave you with a reminder." The man's breath was laden with alcohol and cigarette smoke. "Just remember your agreement."

The burly assailant slammed another fist to his

face, and Jeremy felt a tear above his eye split open. Blood rushed down his face and into his mouth. Jeremy's knees slowly crumbled. The man hopped into a silver car and sped away.

Should've expected this. Should've expected to never get out. Jeremy leaned against the SUV tire and succumbed to the darkness flooding his eyes.

20

Selena let the soaring temperatures of the Texas sun touch the cold spots buried inside her. Her anxiety left spiky nuggets of apprehension up and down her back. Now, the heat burrowed into her soul reminding her of happy childhood times and days spent in its warmth. Home; her safe haven. Papá's ranch. Safe from DeNickey's advances and Jeremy's confusing statements.

Patches, sprawled asleep on his blanket for the last fifty miles, stood and stretched.

"Wait." Selena told him, palm up, his signal to stay until she was ready for him to leave the car.

Selena picked up the Sprite she'd bought along the way and took a long sip. Frowning at the slight nausea still present, she popped the trunk and slid out a small duffle bag with her clothing.

Selena peeked over the hatchback and saw a brown and white fur ball race to her. Patches barked a greeting as Cookie, the resident farm dog, raced around to the open door, planted front feet on the seat and whined.

"Cookie." Selena shouted as Jolie bustled to the car to see the commotion.

Selena grabbed Cookie's collar and yanked him out of the vehicle.

"Oh, Dios mio. I didn't know you'd have a dog with you. I would have kept him in the house." Jolie said, grabbing the scruff of Cookie's neck.

"I didn't want to leave him at home with a sitter. I think they'll be fine once they're introduced." Selena slipped the lead on Patches and released him from the back seat.

"Mercy." Jolie still held the panting Cookie, his excitement dripping on her well-worn shoes.

"Cookie, meet Patches." Selena patted the large puppy and encouraged Patches to sniff and make friends. Patches looked gently at the bouncing ball of energy. He eyed the strangers and the surroundings, circled three times, and dropped to the ground with a loud sigh.

"Wow. I expected more of a reaction." Jolie commented. "Should I let Cookie go? He's liable to jump right up and chew on her ear."

Selena laughed at the image. "I don't think Patches cares one way or another."

Cookie, freed, jumped on Selena, knocking her off balance and into the dirt. Patches stood and joined Cookie in licking Selena's face.

"My word. What kind of dog is he? He's huge." Jolie exclaimed, watching the puppy, a great deal larger than the cow dog.

"He's a Newfoundland- Labrador mix from the shelter. Isn't he gorgeous?" Selena wiped her face free of the tongue bath.

"And his name is Patches? He has all those different colors in his fur. And the white parts are almost blinding. He's beautiful." Jolie bent down to scratch the puppy's tummy, while Cookie chewed on Selena's boots,

"Grace!"

Selena smiled, hearing her middle name, and turned to her father. "Papá."

"I have missed you, hija,"

A sharp pain raced across her face.

"Hearing you call me Grace took me back a few years. You know I'll be 25 soon."

"You'll always be Grace to me." Papá hugged her neck and kissed the top of her head.

"Walk me to the barn." Watching Patches and Cookie nose each other under Jolie's careful eye, Selena entwined her arm with her father's.

"Look. The cowboys are starting to roll in." Papá pointed at the thin cloud of dust on a hill near the ranch. The Western Action Shooting event included various competitions with cowboys in themed courses of shooting for time and accuracy. "Are you going to compete? I can get She'Daisy from the pasture."

"I don't know yet. My costume is still here, if I can fit into it, and I'm sure I could borrow the same guns from last time I competed." Selena looked forward to riding She'Daisy, her beautiful ranch horse. She'Daisy had been a cattle horse until Selena claimed her, now she was content to eat in the pasture until Selena's next visit. "If Ben's competing, I'll need to see about competing against him, too. At least in the mounted competition." Ben, the rancher's son was as important to her as She'Daisy. Both brought fond memories of her childhood.

Selena touched the side of her throbbing head. The pains were coming sharper and more painful. She knew she would be unable to function if she didn't take medicine soon.

"Headache?" Papá asked, hand-motioning to a spigot on the side of the barn.

"Yes." Selena smiled at the memory of leaning under the well pump and asking Papá or Ben to pump the ice-cold water over her head and neck. It was drastic measures but only provided a small respite. "I'm not sticking my head under the spigot. Let's walk around first. I've got water in the car."

"Come. You can walk around later after you've rested." Papá linked arms again and led her back to the car. Patches had found quiet ground under a lilac bush and was gently chasing rabbits in his sleep.

Selena grabbed her tote with the meds and followed her father up onto the wraparound porch. Papá stepped inside, grabbed a cold bottle of water and returned to the twin rocker next to Selena's.

Selena took a big swallow and chased the medication down. Crickets chirped as Selena heard Jolie giving directions in the kitchen.

"Still get those headaches."

"Not so much. It's been a long week." Selena peeked one eye open at him. She knew he didn't like her working at the prison. If he had a say in her choices, she would be right here on the ranch.

"I don't know why..."

"Papá, please. We've been over this. I like this job. It's just some days, or weeks, are worse than others."

Papá stood and patted her knee. "You rest. I'll

go check on dinner and then we'll take a drive over to town and see how things are shaping up there."

After an hour in the shadow of the porch, Selena joined the other cowhands for supper in the spacious kitchen. Jolie, knowing her favorite foods, had outdone herself with steak, baked potatoes, and chocolate cake.

Selena listened as the cowhands talked work and about the cattle and the weekend affair. She grinned, mouth full of buttery biscuits, at the friendly banter with her father and the rancher.

"Thank you, Jolie. Although I may not be able to fit in my costume tomorrow." Selena winced thinking about how snug the pants had been last year. She stood and helped clear the table.

"With that scrawny, little figure? You should have eaten more." Jolie kissed her on the cheek, leftovers in one hand and dirty dishes in the other. "Now, shoo. Stand there too long and I'll have you elbow-deep in the sink."

"I love you, Jolie. Even if you call me scrawny." Selena said as she scooted out of the kitchen. Jolie was the foundation at the ranch, well respected and highly esteemed. Jolie's deep alto voice floated through the air singing "Jesus knows me, this I love," her rendition of the Bible song.

Selena motioned for Patches to jump in the back and hopped into her father's big work truck. In one flying, furry leap, Patches landed and then proudly hung his head over the side, nose in the air.

"He acts like he's done this before." Papá smiled at her. They could see Cookie already racing towards town, dust flying behind her. The truck crossed through back pastures, a low-slung gate, and along the edge of an irrigation lake. A well-worn dirt road branched off to the west and a more defined gravel road to the south.

"I don't think I remember seeing that road. Where does it go?" Selena pointed. Barbed wire fencing spread on either side of a padlocked gate a hundred yards down from where they stopped.

"A boys ranch. Mark Bruens turned it into a ranch where boys who have been court ordered to live away from home can stay. Sad, but true. I don't know if they have criminal pasts, or what. Mark doesn't or can't share any information. I know there's never been any violence. In fact, Mark raises livestock for the boys to take care of, gives them a sense of responsibility, so he says. And we invite the boys over from time to time to work an event on the ranch or the western shooting competition. We haven't had any problems." Papá adjusted his cowboy hat. "Do you remember the Bruens?"

"No, I never knew them. I knew there was a house back there under the trees and a ranch next door, but nothing else. I think they had boys several years older than me."

"Good people. Maybe you'll meet them sometime."

Selena and her father pulled up next to the post office, a prefabricated building, to check in with the competition coordinator. A variety of horses stood at the saloon, swishing flies with their long tails.

Caroline, the town's "mayor" and competition coordinator, glanced up as they walked through the rough-hewn door to the post office. Sepia-stained photos of long passed criminals were posted on the wall next to a "We Shoot First" sign. In full costume as required by the Western Shooting Association rules, Caroline shook their hands, her hat pushed hard down on her head. Her clunky spurs clicked on the wooden floorboards as she reached out to them.

"Evening, Manuel. Welcome back, Selena. Your father said you might be here for this one." Caroline shook Selena's hand.

"Wow, look at you. Fringe and all."

Caroline spun in a half circle, so Selena could see the entire outfit. The buckskin jacket and prairie skirt accented Caroline's curvy figure.

"Are you signing up for anything?"

"The mounted shooting event with She'Daisy." Selena signed her name under Ben's. Mounted shooting was her best sport and her favorite, but she also signed her name under Ben's on the Jail Break competition. Surely, she could still beat Ben shooting steel knock-down targets. "Also, the Jail Break. Ben still thinks he can beat me. I guess I need to show him who's who around here. Again."

"You may get a run for your money." Caroline stepped back behind the counter, gathered Selena's entrance papers, and nodded to Papá. "See you tomorrow."

Selena and Manuel left the post office and walked the half block, down past the bakery, with sweet smelling, yeasty goodies, to the livery on the far edge of town. The old barn-looking structure held what most liveries in the past would hold, stables of horses and storage rooms for tack. A young boy sat outside the red, double doors, chewing a piece of gum. Manuel tipped his hat at him and winked as they walked farther down around the corrals.

"Potter's son," he said, nodding to the boy who was still watching them. "He likes to watch the people comin' and goin'. Best place for that kind of watchin'."

"Is he from the boy's ranch?"

"No. Putter is the livery manager. His son lives with him."

Selena turned back to the child and saw a man turn quickly and walk away from them. Odd, almost as if he didn't want to run into her. All she could see was the black hat, but he had a gait that looked very familiar. One of the cow hands, maybe? Or maybe it didn't have anything to do with her. A tiny knot of apprehension slithered its way up her neck.

21

Suzie hung her jacket and purse on the hook inside the prison locker and put the small key in her jeans. In the corner, a large black woman sat dabbing her eyes and patting the baby in her arms.

Seated on the long row of torn chairs across from her was a young woman with dyed black hair, a heavily made-up face, and meanness in her eyes. Caught staring openly at the woman, Suzie was greeted with a hiss.

She glanced at the guard sitting behind Plexiglas and stood when her name was called. Stepping behind a partition, Suzie was quickly searched by a female guard. Fat hands lifted her arms to half-mast, and a metal detector wand was passed over every inch of her body. The guard gestured with a grunt and a wave toward the open door. She knew what she looked like: stylishly faded jeans, tight blouse, gold glittering around her neck and fingers. She looked like a hooker, an upscale hooker, of course, but one nonetheless. And decidedly not unmemorable like Brandon requested at their last visit. He might be upset with her, but it wouldn't be the first time.

The guard waved her on and Suzie strode past

her with a smirk.

"Hey, it's my favorite girl." Brandon sat down at her table. He raised eyebrows at her outfit, laughed at her teased hair.

"Better be your only one, don't ya think?" She wished she had gum to smack. Suzie looked him over. "I promised I wouldn't come as a bag lady."

"True, but this will definitely create an impression on anyone and everyone watching us." Brandon chided her.

"If you can be undercover, so can I."

"And what are you posing as?"

"Your old lady, of course. How's it going?"

"Just the usual. Trying to keep my head clear. You know, the parties in here are wild, the women wilder." Brandon laughed.

Suddenly, Suzie bent at the waist, checking the floor. Brandon glanced quickly at the guards who hadn't noticed her unexpected movement.

"Suzie. Suz. Are you alright?" he whispered.

Suzie changed position in her chair, pulling long bangs over her face. Trying to be nonchalant, she looked over her shoulder at the guard and then down the long hallway through the glass.

"That was him!" Suzie said.

"Him, who?"

"Last night I went to the bar…don't say it…just let me finish." Suzie put her hands in front of her, willing him not to speak. "There was a fat guy sitting at the bar with a floozy, and I wasn't paying much attention to him, just drinking my…" Suzie, noticing his frown, resisted the urge to punch him. "Wait, just let me finish, will ya?"

"Anyway, the guy that went down the hall," Suzie gestured with her eyes. "He was the fat guy."

"So?"

"Another guy came in, a good-looking guy by the way, and they were talking about your little guard friend, Maldanado."

"Suzie. First, of all," Brandon started. "She's not my guard friend. Secondly, you know what I've been doing."

Suzie's shoulders slumped. "I know."

"Don't question that. If anything, please don't question me. You know there are some ugly things going on, and I may have to get ugly, too. You knew that."

"Okay, okay. Don't you want to know what they were saying?"

"Of course."

"Well, apparently the good-looking one is her boyfriend." Suzie slanted her eyes at Brandon. "You know she has a boyfriend?"

"Yes, you mentioned him last time we talked."

"Just shut up for a minute, will ya?" Suzie pulled her tresses back again. "Anyway, they were talking about Maldanado, and dope was mentioned several times."

"Dope, how? Like she's such a dope? Or she's carrying dope in?"

"Drugs, you idiot."

"Oh. Well, we thought she was connected. What do you think?" Brandon squinted his eyes.

"I think you know more about her than you started with. I know we can tie Maldanado to the FBI agent, and now we can connect him to the investigator. The three together have to be working it somehow." Suzie held up three fingers indicating the connection between them.

~

Brandon, along with the guards, watched Suzie walk from the visiting room.

Lord, I sure hope you're watching all of this because it could get nasty really quick. Brandon prayed silently. Loneliness swelled over him. Suzie was a rollercoaster of emotions at this visit which was unlike her normal level-headedness. He needed her stable and not hopping from one foot to the other with anxiety. The maintenance wore him out. Disappointment was a close second. The connection between the three of them had been confirmed.

Still wrestling with his thoughts, Brandon headed over to the small room the Prison Fellowship group used as a chapel. No one else was there, so he took a chair against the wall and sat, head down.

"Good evening. Chapel isn't tonight although you're welcome to stay." A tall, elderly man entered the room, his arms full of pamphlets.

Brandon recognized him from past prison fellowship meetings. He looked like someone's grandfather with his thinning, gray hair, and wooden fingers, stiff with arthritis. The man still stood by Brandon's chair but curled a hand around the metal back to steady himself.

Somehow, this man got the short end of the stick. Like one of those so-called myths, "If you get saved, God will send you to the jungles of Africa." Apparently, He sent this guy to the prisoners, a different jungle of sorts. Brandon sensed a calmness in the man that he, himself, didn't possess. His words seemed consistent with his actions as if he enjoyed talking to the inmates and always cared about their eternal decisions.

"Wayne Trichler, and your name?" The man pulled a chair alongside Brandon, his Visitor ID swinging outside his sweater. Mr. Trichler held a small book Brandon recognized as a Gideon Bible from the prison library. He wasn't familiar with the Gideons, but thought they must be good people, leaving Bibles wherever they went.

"Brandon." He shifted in his seat, so the old man could see him better and wouldn't stretch his neck out. "I've been here before, during chapel time, when you were here."

"Oh, well, been coming here for almost twenty years. Thought I would drop off pamphlets and make sure the room is ready for tomorrow." Clear, blue eyes behind bi-focals studied Brandon's face. "Why did you come here?"

"Actually, I'm doing a little wrestling. I feel like I'm wrestling with God right now." Between Suzie, Maldanado, and everyday prison life. Brandon felt his focus slipping away.

Mr. Trichler laughed. "Son, that's a good place to be. Let me know if I can help. I'm not good at the wrestling, a couple of tussles occasionally, but I've had my fair share of letting God win." He got up from the chair, carefully, and used the backs of other chairs scattered across the room to keep his balance.

"I usually ask my wife to type up the notes since my handwriting is bad," Mr. Trichler continued to hold the chalk unsteadily. "But she died recently."

Ouch. And he's here concerned about inmates. Brandon kept his head low, unsure if he should say anything. "I'm sorry," he finally whispered.

"Me, too." Mr. Trichler said, still facing the chalkboard.

Life was already emotional enough for Brandon; he didn't need to take on some old man's loss as well. But when Mr. Trichler took out his handkerchief and wiped his eyes, Brandon felt moisture in his own.

22

After a decent night sleep in her old bed at the ranch, Selena woke and dressed, grateful for a reprieve from yesterday's pounding headache. Stretch jeans were supposed to have give, weren't they? Selena tossed her wild mane back.

She stuck her hat on, and with a couple of deep knee bends to stretch out the jeans, she went downstairs. Her first competition was in a couple of hours. Only the faintest of uncertainty clung to her after yesterday's walk with her father and the cowboy who had quickly walked away from her.

"Ready to ride, I see?" Jolie met her on the landing. She smelled of fresh baked bread and herbs.

"Yeah, I want to get there before Ben does. He still thinks he can beat me." Selena smiled, adjusting the holster on her slender hips.

"He's getting good. He's a good boy, you know." Jolie winked at her.

"I'm sure he is. Any brother of mine better be." Selena bent and kissed the older woman's cheek. As Selena and Ben had grown up and gone their separate ways, Jolie often commented they weren't really blood relatives. Selena suspected Ben would have been Jolie's favored choice for a relationship with Selena.

Ben was her closest friend on the ranch, certainly not relationship material.

As she reached the barn, Selena ran into the man himself.

"Well, if it isn't Sally. Sweet Seat Sally. Maybe I should just call you Sweet Sally." Ben grabbed her in a bear hug, unmindful of the stares from the other cowboys saddling up. Her position at the ranch had always been an unknown. She was their boss' daughter, but not "The Boss' daughter". Tied to the family but not by blood. They did, however, treat her with respect as she could ride and shoot better than most men. Selena liked it that way, true acceptance and appreciation for her ability and talent.

"You're up early? I figured you'd still be wiping the sleep out of your eyes."

Selena hugged him back. The teasing felt great after long stressful days at the prison. Sometimes she felt more confined than the inmates did.

"It's Long-Shootin' Joe to you now. You'll see my name in the winner's circle every time."

"Ha. I think you're mistaken. IF your name is on the board, it will be below mine."

Selena whistled low and was rewarded with a nicker from She'Daisy. She still knew the sound of Selena's voice. Grabbing a brightly colored blanket, She'Daisy's bridle and saddle, Selena brought the horse out to the center of the barn. Always ready to go, She'Daisy pranced sideways as Selena saddled her and slid the bridle over the horse's twitching ears.

She cinched up the saddle and hiked her foot

over the horn. Anxious to get out into the fresh air, She'Daisy galloped out of the barn as soon as Selena's boots adjusted in the stirrups. The sun shining on the nearby pond and the feel of She'Daisy running underneath her brought a smile.

Entering the streets of the little town, She'Daisy slowed and walked next to Ben's horse, who'd arrived at the same time.

Selena closed her eyes and let the sea of smells ride over her. Fried chicken from the saloon, dust kicked up by the horses, sun-kissed leather, and gun smoke filled the air. The closer she got to the arenas on the far side, the clearer she could hear the sounds of competition. Shots rang out in single file with only half seconds in between.

Watching an old cowboy walk away from her, she thought about the guy she'd spotted earlier. The gait had looked familiar. Jeremy? Out here?

She turned She'Daisy out onto the dirt track and shifted her seating as the horse side-stepped in anticipation of another run. She'd walk her for a bit, get the jitters out, and then walk through the competition route.

"Whooeee!" a hat slapped her thigh and She'Daisy skittered.

"Hey." Selena called after the rider. Slapping the reins, she let the horse take its head and catch up to the other horse. "BEN!"

Selena gained control of She'Daisy and raced after Ben's tall quarter horse. She gave Ben a lopsided grin as she pulled She'Daisy back into the staging area. "That was fun."

"Keep control of your mount, cowgirl." Ben

smiled back at her. "You're on deck. Let me show you how this is done."

The announcer called Ben, or Long Shootin' Joe, to the starting line.

Ben rode fast, shot all of his targets except one, and finished in record time. Selena's run, however, was a rough one and Ben waited in the back lot for her.

"Been a while." Selena dusted off her hat and blew out a breath.

"I know. Maybe you'll be better at the Jail Break? Hmm, maybe not." Ben rode easily beside her. "I need the points to make it to the semi-finals or I would have let you win."

"Uh, huh. We'll see." Good possibility he'd win that one, too, but the banter and riding were what she really had come home for. Ben should win, and he should get the opportunity to ride in the semi-finals. Maybe she'd let him. Selena coughed into her elbow. She'd never in her life let someone beat her.

Ben and Selena dismounted and handed their reins over to Mr. Potter.

"We'll be out for a while, Mr. Potter. Our next event isn't with the horses." Ben shook the old man's grizzly hand. "Maybe your son can unsaddle them for us?"

"Sure thing, Mr. Ben. He'd be happy, too. We'll take good care of them. If, by chance, it's later than you expect, I'll put your horses in a stall for the night, and you can settle up in the morning." Mr. Potter disappeared into the inner stables, leading both horses to a corner lot.

"Where's his son? Papá and I passed him

yesterday when I first got here." Selena asked, noticing the empty watching spot.

"Probably on another stoop looking at the people. He's a good boy, but he watches everything like he's recording it in his brain. Sometimes it feels a little weird."

"Huh." Selena thought about Mr. Potter's son. They'd passed him when that man had turned and walked away from them. Maybe Mr. Potter's son had seen him, too. Or maybe Ben had. "Ben, hey, hadn't told you this yet, but I've been kinda seeing someone." Or at least seeing a lot more of him than she thought she would.

Ben looked sideways at her. "You wanna walk over to the Jail Break comp?"

"Yes. I know you'll probably beat me, but walking would be good. Anyway, I thought I might have seen him here yesterday." Selena shrugged, knowing she wasn't making sense.

Ben stopped walking. "You mean, he might have been here, but didn't say anything to you about coming here?"

"Yes, well, no." She looked more stupid by the minute. "I thought I saw him, but when he didn't look around like he was trying to find me, I thought it probably wasn't him. But it really looked like him and then I started getting creeped out thinking he was here but didn't want me to know he was here."

"Sounds more like a stalker than a boyfriend." Ben moved down the boardwalk shaking hands with people he knew.

"Well, yes, if it was him. And he's not really a boyfriend. But now I've blabbed all over myself, I'm thinking I've got some marbles loose. He'd never do that."

"Why? Because he loves you?" Ben made kissy-noises in the air.

"Don't be juvenile. He's just not creepy."

"Then why didn't you bring him?"

"Because I wanted to get away." Selena opened the gate to the spectator section. "And I don't want the pressure."

"Sounds like a creepy, stalker-boyfriend to me." Ben picked up his guns and moved through the next gate. Selena followed, nodding at the range master.

"He is not. It's been a long week, and I'm tired, and I want to let my guard down for half a second."

They stopped in the staging area and watched the other competitors run through the gamut. Shoot through the bars at the bad guys, avoid shooting the pop-up steel spectators, run for the bag of gold while shooting at more bad guys. It was a fun, fast-paced set up as the timer recorded times.

"Get your guns and then we'll talk more about your stalker."

"Ben…" Selena quieted as Ben checked in with the range master, presented his guns for inspection, and prepared to compete. Minutes later, it was her turn.

~

After lots of laughs with other cowboys in the competition and a great hamburger at the saloon, Selena walked out to the barn to check on She'Daisy. She'd stayed later than expected, and Ben had turned in earlier.

She'Daisy was eating a pile of hay and appeared

content to stay the night. Ben's big gelding wasn't in the barn, and she suspected he'd ridden it home. Putter's boy had indeed unsaddled She'Daisy and fed and watered the horse. Selena unclicked the lead rope from the halter and let it swing down the stall door, banging against the bottom bars. The clanging metal startled some of the other horses in the otherwise quiet barn.

"Sorry, girl, but I'm not walking home in the dark by myself." Selena hefted the saddle onto the horse and tightened down all of the straps. She'Daisy was not in any hurry to leave her hay. "I know, I know. You were settling in, but you've still got work to do. I'll even sing to you on the way home."

Noting the door to the small office area was ajar, Selena decided to leave a note for Mr. Potter and settle up his services. Pulling money out of her pocket, she settled into an old creaky chair on rollers. There was enough light from the outside lights to push through the darkness and allow her to see the bills in her hand and to scratch out a note. A table in the corner held pieces of broken tack someone was repairing.

The cough behind her caused Selena to jump from the chair.

"Sorry, I didn't know anyone was in here, and the light was off..." Selena whirled around.

A growing dread settled in her stomach and began weaving its way up her throat. Selena assessed the distance to the door. The man, slim built with a cowboy hat on, remained in the corner.

She'Daisy was outside the office, saddled and ready. Could she make it to her? The flight or fight sensation was resting heavily on her chest now. Her heartbeat began to speed up. Why hadn't the man said anything when she'd first come in? Why was he in there with the light off? None of this equaled a friendly encounter.

"Selena." His voice shattered her thoughts.

"Jeremy?"

23

Brandon looked down from his bunk as the cell door was unlocked from the outside. He usually left his door open, but he needed quiet time. He'd thought long and hard about his conversation with Mr. Trichler, and it still left a bitter taste in his mouth.

Truth was freedom, it wasn't as easy as it sounded. His whole life had been about truth in an upside-down kind of way. There hadn't been an escape route in some of his situations. If everything worked out the way he expected it to, the truth would be revealed, and he could walk away justified. There was the second word Mr. Trichler had written on the board...Justify. Just as if he'd never done it. Although the saying was nice and the thought of being free was comforting, it probably wasn't realistic. He'd never be free of the guilt he felt over certain things he'd done.

"Hey, I need help with some files up in Maldanado's office." Sam filled his doorway. "More inmates coming in. You got time?" Sam glanced at the handmade posters on the walls. One-word signs in elaborate script were taped to the wall. Faith,

Hope, and Obey were sketched on the papers.

"Sure." He had nowhere to be. Maybe he could pick up useful information about the little drug threesome. Brandon shook the thoughts out of his head and pulled gray state-issued pants over his shorts.

Big drops of rain fell as they walked side by side to the administration building.

Sam glanced at him as he unlocked the door.

"You can wait in here while I get the files from Receiving. Don't touch anything. You shouldn't even be in here." Sam hurried into the office; large wet spots dotted his dress shirt.

Brandon put his fingers up in the traditional Boy Scout salute. "I promise I'll stay right here."

With a second glance at him, Sam pulled the interior door open and walked out to Receiving. Brandon could see him occasionally through the partially glass walls, gathering files and paperwork from a nearby desk.

With another look to see where Sam was, he scanned the desk, looking for items that might be of use to him. At some point, he was going to tangle with the woman. He could swipe something, something small, for leverage. A staff's personal property found in an inmate's room would look like theft on his side but could also lean toward inappropriate behavior on her part, leaving doubt as a resonating factor.

Finding something to take off Maldanado's desk and hide in his room would only be insurance if he needed it. A guilt pang settled in his gut. He really wanted the investigator, the dirty one, not

Maldanado. He was sure she was caught in this web and not a part of it, but with no way to prove it yet, he had to move forward and catch whoever he could. He had to separate his mind from his actions and do what was necessary.

Brandon carefully inched toward the waist-high bookcase where several trinkets sat with framed pictures. He bent over to look at the pictures. Most were of sunrises, red clay hills, tall pines surrounding lakes. No family pictures. Did she have family nearby? Single, he knew that much. A small, flat silver frame caught his eye. Maldanado with a beautiful gray horse. Dropping it inside his shirt, Brandon felt it lay heavily against his belt. If the guards searched him on the way back, they'd feel it but Brandon didn't think they would since he was with Sam.

"Here are the files." Sam came back in, carrying several large manila folders.

Brandon carried the files close to his body, disguising the lump in the front of his shirt, as they hurried back to the housing unit. They passed through the guard check with the guard casually waving to Sam. After stopping at Sam's office, Brandon headed back to his room. Hunched over in the rain, he felt exposed as if everyone knew he was carrying contraband in his shirt. Very few inmates were out on the yard, so he only had to get past the guards in his housing unit.

It would be a sorry day if he had to use the picture for leverage, but it was there if he had to. Brandon stuffed the small frame into a small cut in his mattress. Lying on his bunk, he thought about his next move. All his plans circled around Maldanado, the long-legged investigator.

Maldanado. In another time and space, he would have pursued her, at least to get to know her better. She was cocky, beautiful, and should be enjoying the good things of life, not stuck inside a corrections institution. He watched her school her face into a blank slate with no emotion peeking out. What would her laugh be like? Her home life, with her stretched out on her couch, at ease? Brandon longed to get the picture back out and study it. Study her smile. Nope, stay focused on the plan. He couldn't, wouldn't, follow the What Ifs. They just weren't in the cards.

24

"Selena." Jeremy took a step toward her.

"Jeremy? How did you get here?" Selena's brow furrowed. "Why? Why are you here?" Her feet refused to move. To the door or to him?

"I needed to talk. With you." Jeremy came closer. An outdoor lamp shone in the window, displaying his swollen lip and blackened eye.

"Oh mi Dios. What happened?" Selena flipped the switch, flooding the room with light. Meeting him in the center, she took inventory of the scratches and bruises on his face. A laceration across his eyebrow made her wince. "Jeremy, what happened?"

Taking her hand in his, he said, "I got jumped."

"By who? When?"

"After I'd been to your place."

"But how? You're FBI." Selena walked him over to the chair and turned him to face her.

Jeremy snorted. "Yeah, we're superhuman."

"Well, no, you know what I meant. Usually, you're aware of everything. To get jumped?" Selena thought back to the self-defense class where she'd nearly broken his nose. Her only advantage had been surprise.

"It happened." Jeremy shrugged his shoulders.

"Who would do this?" He probably had a handful of enemies who would gladly take a shot at him. Maybe one of them had caught up with Jeremy.

"I don't know."

"Did you call the cops?"

"Uh, no. FBI, remember? I'm not calling them."

"We'll figure it out. How did you find me? You know, I saw you here on the ranch earlier." She hoped his response was a good one.

"FBI again. After what happened to me, I wanted to make sure you were safe."

"Why hide from me? Why not just call and say, 'Guess what, I'm here.'" Selena bit her bottom lip. There were holes in his story. Was he making it up as he went?

"I saw you were okay, so I was going to turn around and leave. Then I couldn't without saying something. And look at me? Wouldn't everyone be a little concerned about the guy who got his face rearranged walking around with you?"

Selena arched her eyebrows and frowned. "Probably. I was planning on going home tomorrow morning. How did you get here?"

"I drove out. I'm leaving tonight. As long as you're okay, there's no reason to stay around." Jeremy stood, allowing her to help him out of the chair. "Listen, can we talk when you get back?"

"Yeah, I'll call you." Selena let go of his hand.

Stepping closer, Jeremy quickly kissed her forehead and left.

Selena stood, rooted to the spot where he'd left her. So many thoughts tangling with each other; his soft kiss high on the list. Stalker boyfriend, Ben's words, a close second.

25

Selena started her Monday morning looking for a coke, coffee, or something to jumpstart her head. A sleepless night with too much pensive thinking was going to bring on another migraine.

"I wanna talk to you. In my office. Now." DeNickey growled at Selena.

And that would bring one on, too. Selena turned and followed her boss.

Selena pulled on her nonchalant mask over her feelings and prepared herself for whatever DeNickey was upset about.

Suddenly, DeNickey's gruffness ended, and his syrupy sweet talk began. "I hear the party is at your house this weekend? And I didn't get invited?"

What party? The poker party? How did he hear about the poker parties? She could bluff. Her heart started thudding in her chest.

He wouldn't be invited if he were the only… Selena's thoughts started to swirl. Who was at the last poker party at her house? Jeremy, Sam, a couple of the third shift guards.

"No." Give as little information as possible. Only answer direct questions. Selena used

DeNickey's own interview tactics.

"Not this weekend, huh? How about past parties?"

"No, not this weekend. Yes, to the past parties. You didn't get your invitation?"

Selena doubted her smart aleck comment would affect his tirade. It might even incite his questioning.

"Ha." DeNickey snorted. "Who was at your last one? Surely, they are invited to the next one."

Selena's stomach flipped over. Why was he interested in who came over? Who was he gunning for?

"Why? You keepin' tabs on everyone's parties now?"

"Do not mess with me." DeNickey's tone lowered. He was steamed up about something, and Selena would be the last one to feed him any information.

"Look, if there's something going on. . . Some of the people who came to the party work here, and some don't." That much was true. Maybe if she gave a tiny morsel of information, he'd back off.

"I asked you a direct question." DeNickey came around his desk and leaned on the front. "I can either get the information from you, or I can get it other ways. I can guarantee you won't like the other ways. Neither will your invitees."

Selena scrambled for a response.

"I'm waiting." DeNickey crossed his arms and bore a hole through her forehead.

"Well, you know Jeremy was there." Selena tried to keep eye contact with him.

"Ah, yes, Jeremy. Let's talk about him for a

moment."

He knew Jeremy would be there.

"Okay." Selena drew the word out, giving her time to think. "What do you want with Jeremy?" Selena thought of Jeremy's beating, definitely bad vibes coming from both Jeremy and DeNickey now.

"I've just noticed things here and there. How close you two are, how often he shows up at the prison now. Are you dating?"

Selena refused to answer.

"You know he's bad news, don't you?" DeNickey reached out and touched her knee. "You could find someone better."

DeNickey was a stinking, rotten, ugly thing posing as a human. Selena fumed. In one sentence, he had degraded her almost boyfriend and put his slimy thoughts and hands on her. Selena narrowed her eyes, pressing her lips tightly together.

"Oh, I see I've insulted you. Well, as your boss," DeNickey stressed the word, "I thought you should know he's trouble and to watch your back. Now, if you want to know any of his dirty, little secrets, you just come see me, and we'll have a private lunch in my office and talk. You're dismissed."

Selena left, acid swirling in her mouth. She wanted to lash out and hit him. Hard. Drop-to-the-floor hard. Not where the sun didn't shine but until the sun didn't shine anymore.

~

Selena set her purse down and scratched Patches behind the ear. A wet spot on the couch was evidence from where he'd laid all day. Selena sighed. Wouldn't it be nice to be a dog and lay around?

DeNickey had almost sent her around the bend with his fruitless questioning. She still had no idea what the interrogation was about. The advances and uninvited touches were coming more often and bolder, as if Jeremy's appearance in her life was stirring up jealousy in DeNickey. Ick.

The phone rang as Selena pulled items out of the fridge to make an omelet for supper.

"Hello?"

"Hey, I thought you were going to call me when you got home?" Jeremy paused on the other side of the line. Before Selena could answer, Jeremy pressed on. "I'm in the neighborhood and thought I could stop in."

Wow, three times in one week Jeremy had shown up unexpectedly. Stalker came to mind. And in the neighborhood? There wasn't a neighborhood within ten miles of her house.

"Um, sure. How are you feeling?"

The doorbell rang before he responded.

Selena opened the door and narrowed her eyes at Jeremy standing just outside the house with his cell phone to his ear.

"Wow, you really were in the neighborhood." Selena eyed his face, noting the black bruises fading to green on the outer edges.

"Are we standing outside for a reason?"

"No, come in. Sorry I didn't call right away. There's a lot going on." Selena led the way to the kitchen.

"Hey, wait. Shouldn't the poor beat up guy get a hug?"

A hug? Selena hesitated.

Wrapping his arms around her waist, Jeremy pulled her to him. She laid her head against his rock-solid chest. Blinking slowly, Selena blew out a breath. There was something so not right about this, and yet, this felt so good. If only the dread and anxiety would shut up.

Letting her go, Jeremy started breaking the eggs into the bowl. She felt the warmth of his body leave with him.

Selena leaned against the counter and watched him take over. Sautéing the onions, scrambling the eggs and adding milk, he looked comfortable in her kitchen.

Jeremy stepped over Patches as he handed her a steaming omelet.

"Have you thought anymore about who did this to your face?" Selena asked with concern.

"Did you see DeNickey today? How was he?"

"What do you mean 'How was he?' Funny thing, he and I had a pretty heated conversation about you today. You're asking about him, and he's asking about you?" Selena sat down at the kitchen table and waited for an answer. His coat was behind her, and she could faintly smell his cologne on the jacket. Turning her fork over and over, clanking it against the knife, she watched him.

"I think DeNickey put out the beat down."

Selena's fork clattered to the floor. "Why?" Having someone beat up? Was that possible for DeNickey? And why Jeremy? "Why?"

Jeremy set his uneaten plate on the counter and scooted a chair up beside her. "Selena, look at me."

She didn't want to. He was about to tell her what

she was dreading, the why behind the unaccounted anxiety.

"I've done some things. Bad things." Jeremy started, leaning towards her.

Selena slid her chair against the wall, feeling the weight of his jacket swing with the movement. He must have his concealed carry weapon in it. "Haven't we all?"

"Sure, but mine involves DeNickey." Jeremy took her hand, holding it tighter when she tried to pull it away.

"DeNickey's scum. Why would you do anything with him?" Selena wrapped her other arm around her waist and then let it drop by her side, hanging.

"Do you remember when I said it might not be you those convicts were referring to when they brought up the investigator's office and drugs? It's DeNickey. And this outside source? I'm his supplier."

26

"His supplier?" Selena sat back in her chair, breath absent from her chest. "Meaning what? You supply drugs to the prison?" Stomach acid began to inch upwards toward her throat. The walls of the room moved in, closer, stifling.

Jeremy held onto her hand as he stared into her eyes. No hint of malice or violence, just simply a confession.

"Yes." A one-word answer from him. "Although there are others involved, too, inside and outside the prison."

Selena tried to wrap her head around his statement. He'd told her he was committing a felony, confessed it out right. The lines on his face were etched in yellow, adding to the purple and green bruises. Why?

Selena scooted her chair back with a scrape and stood, jerking her hand from his. Jeremy stood with her. And to think she'd enjoyed his touch earlier. She wanted to spit on him now.

"You're in with DeNickey, the guy you've claimed to be disgusted with. And you're selling drugs. Into the prison." Selena took a step back, closer to the coffee table.

With a lunge, Selena pulled open the coffee table drawer, clicked the safety off her gun and leveled it at him. The second time she'd pointed a weapon at him. But this one was loaded.

~

"Whoa. Put it away and let's talk." He'd handled the situation all wrong. He should have started with something else, like talk about his sick sister.

"Not a chance. Get out." Selena slit her eyes at him.

"And then what? You know I can't leave with you having knowledge of DeNickey and me." Jeremy moved to the sofa and sat on the edge.

"You can. If you want to see the sun come up tomorrow. You'll leave now."

Selena kept her back to the door, the barrel wavering in her hands.

"Can't do that. Selena, why do you think I told you?"

"Because I was about to find out. Or maybe because you thought I was too stupid to figure it out." He noticed her shaky voice, watched the fear parade across her forehead.

"No. Because I need you." Jeremy shook his head and then focused on a small spot on the floor.

"Are you loco? What kind of crap is that? You need me?" Tears started to slide down her face.

In one swift movement, Jeremy charged her and wrestled her to the floor. The gun clattered to the floor and slid under the table. Bucking like a wild bronco and scratching at his arms, his legs, any skin available, she fought him. With his body weight, he forced her to lay flat on her stomach, hands to the side.

Breathing in her ear, he said, "Let's talk for a minute, okay? Let me talk." If he let her up now, it would be tough to get her back to a submissive position. "If I get off, will you stay still for a minute?"

Selena screamed. Putting his hand over her mouth and out of the way of her gnashing teeth, Jeremy pushed a knee into her kidneys. "Selena, I swear, this could go easier. If you scream again…."

Jeremy slid handcuffs from his pocket, brought her arms up together and clicked the metal bracelets on her wrists.

"Now, I'm going to let you up, and you are not going to scream. No one can hear you, it wouldn't do any good, and you will get hurt if you do." Jeremy threatened. He slowly released his hand from her face and waited. Silence, like he wanted. Jeremy pulled her over into a seated position with her back against the door. She hated him. Tears continued to flow down her face. He could see how much she detested him. And she was afraid. He'd put her in this position, between himself and DeNickey. He should never have shown an interest in her.

"Selena…" Jeremy started.

"Don't ever say my name again." Selena growled at him, disheveled and looking more and more like a wild cat, ready to scratch his eyes out.

"Okay, here's the story. When I'm done, we can talk about what to do now." Jeremy sat cross-legged in front of her.

Selena spit at him.

"Nice." Jeremy took a deep breath and wiped it off his shoe with a Kleenex from his jeans pocket. "I never intended for things to get like this. DeNickey and I have known each other for years. I needed quick cash to help out my sister, and it all just fell into place. Connecting with DeNickey helped pay my sister's hospital bills, so big brother was able to cover her expenses. I hooked him up with some of the guys I worked with undercover; he got to be the big man at the prison. Everything worked out fine until you came along, and then all of a sudden, it didn't make sense."

Jeremy reached out his hand to turn her to look at him but withdrew when she flinched.

"Okay, recently I told DeNickey I wanted out. He's involved too many people, and I can't live like this anymore. Plus, I don't know what to do with you." Jeremy touched his still swollen eyelid. "And he ordered the beat down. As a reminder that I can't get out."

Selena flipped her head back in his direction. "I'm not the stupid one, you are."

"Yes, me. I can take that." Jeremy pushed over, his back was against the door, too. "And that's where you come in. I can get out of this if you help me."

"Of all the . . .? I'm the one in handcuffs, and I can help you? I think you've lost your mind." Selena moved away from him, wrists turned unnaturally.

"I can't take this." Jeremy fished the gun out from under the table and tucked it in the waistband of his pants. He dropped his head into his hands. "Look, I've told you about my sister, and the reason I got involved with DeNickey in the first place. I thought I had control over it and could stop whenever the bills were paid off; but they kept coming, and I kept going." He looked at her and shook his head. Sweat dripped from his forehead.

"You got involved with DeNickey to save your sister. I get it, sort of. Why am I in handcuffs again?" Selena slouched.

"Uh, you pointed a gun at me." Jeremy said, eyebrows raised. He couldn't keep her in handcuffs, didn't really want to. Jeremy blew out a pent-up breath. How could he make her understand? After the cuffs came off?

"You have the gun now. Get me out of these things." Selena jangled the chains.

"Will you listen to me?" he muttered. "Like everything else in my life, this has gotten out of hand."

"Jeremy, please. Let me go."

"Will you? Will you listen for just half a second?"

"Yes, yes. Get me out of these." Selena turned, so the handcuffs were facing him, waiting for him to unlock them.

Jeremy slid the key into the lock and released the hinged cuffs from her wrists. She jumped up. He could see the loathing in her eyes. He waited to see what she was going to do next. It didn't really matter. His whole life was going to pot, literally, anyway. She was standing in front of him, the definition of rage written all over her body.

"You are the lowest, slimiest, worthless . . ." Selena stopped. "You know I'm going to the cops now, right?"

"I don't think so." Still sitting against the door, knees bent, he made a decision. He couldn't control her physically, but there was one little tidbit of information he'd hidden that could manipulate her emotionally. If he was going down, DeNickey was going with him. Unfortunately, maybe Selena, too.

"You don't think so? Are you insane?" Selena looked around, presumably for an object to hit him with.

"I want out of the deal. I didn't get into it to be a drug dealer or a supplier. I was taking care of my family. We can take DeNickey out, and I can leave this mess behind." Jeremy stood and sat on a nearby couch. Good, she was finally listening.

"We?"

"Yes, we. And you will do what I ask because I have information on your family that will cause lots of heartache for you if you don't."

"What are you talking about? There is no 'we,' and there isn't any information out there that could harm my family." Selena stepped closer to the door.

"Here's what you're going to do." Jeremy ignored her question. "All of the pot confiscated in the evidence room from the last six months is mine…or DeNickey's…or whoever's you want to call it. I can trace it back to DeNickey based on the quality and well, it may also be laced with other things. I'm not talking about the tea, it was legit. You're going to get some out, plant it on an inmate, I don't care who, and then let authorities know DeNickey is distributing within the prison." Jeremy put his hands on his knees. He needed a drink of water or something stronger.

"I'm going to what? First of all, I'm not doing anything for you, and second of all, that plan is full of holes." Selena laughed, mirthlessly. "What about your involvement in all of this?"

"With DeNickey out of the picture, I'll probably have to disappear for a while so the others involved won't come looking for me."

"You just get away scot free?"

"No, but I can find another way to pay my sister's bills, and I'll be out of the way. You never have to see me again."

"This is crazy. I'm not doing this."

"Yes, you are. As soon as you walk out this door, I'm calling Immigration, will talk to a friend of mine, and start the process of deporting one Manuel Maldanado back to Mexico. When you're successful on your end, I'll halt the proceedings."

Selena stared at him. "My father's illegal?"

27

Selena pulled up in front of the prison and sat with the engine idling. Her sleep had been filled with men in suits with guns chasing her.

"Selena." Sam knocked on her window. "Are you coming in?"

"Yes." Selena stuffed an umbrella and a water bottle into her briefcase and got out, locking the car behind her.

"Long night?" Sam asked.

"Uh, yeah." She pulled a gun on the FBI guy she was at one time attracted to and lost control of the gun. Then she was put in handcuffs. To top that off, he said he was going to use her to set up DeNickey. And if she didn't do what he'd demanded, he'd call INS on her illegal father. Yeah, it was a long night.

The two walked in the building and stepped into the airlock with a female guard. Stuck between two securely air-locked doors with little space to breathe, everyone hurried to accomplish the required duties of signing for radios, showing badges, and submitting to surface searches of their belongings.

The guard opened the female guard's backpack

for their examination. Sam and Selena prepared to bare their own briefcases.

The guards in the control room on the other side of the Plexiglas looked apologetically at Selena and Sam and quietly asked the female guard to submit to a search.

"Officer Jasper?" the guard in the control center acknowledged her. "Can you step out of the airlock please? Maldanado and Matthews, you can proceed."

"You have got to be kidding me. Random search on me?" the guard tossed her backpack on the floor behind Sam and Selena.

"Please unbraid your hair."

Officer Jasper cursed.

"Just procedures."

As they stepped out of the airlock, Selena saw the officer bend at the waist, shake her hair out, vile language exploding from her mouth. A sergeant stepped out of the control room and waved a detecting wand over the woman's hair, her shoes, and her backpack.

"Man, I know that has to be done, but I'd sure hate to be the subject." Sam said, walking behind her on the narrow stairs.

Selena didn't answer. Random searches were naturally disruptive unless she had something to hide. Selena's pulse quickened.

"I need a Diet Coke." Selena dropped her things in the office and walked down the hall.

"First thing this morning? Wow, tough morning." Sam continued to follow her until she stopped in front of the pop machine and punched the Diet Coke button.

"You have no idea." Selena grimaced. How would her closest friend at the prison react if she were caught in a set up? Would Sam believe she'd done it for the right reasons? Were there right reasons? Was protecting her father enough? The fact that Jeremy was in this mess to protect his family didn't go unnoticed.

"Selena. Stop. Can we talk a minute?" After glancing down the hallway, Sam took her arm and guided her in the opposite direction.

Selena let herself be led to her office, silent.

"Why do I get the feeling things aren't right in your life?" Sam didn't allow her to sit at her desk, instead he stopped her inside the doorway. She would feel more in control if she could sit down, behind her own desk where she managed the decisions and their outcomes, where she was in charge.

"What do you mean?" Selena attempted to be nonchalant. "I'm fine."

"I don't think you are. I think you're in over your head with something." Sam searched her face. Just inches from her, he still held on to her forearm. "If I find out it has to do with this Jeremy character, I am going to be livid."

"Jeremy? Why Jeremy?" Selena pulled out of his grasp. Her ears started to burn. "Everything with Jeremy is great." Sweat formed on her face.

"Uh huh. I'm telling you. From what I've observed, you're as tense as a flea on dip day." Sam smiled and put his hand on her shoulder.

Selena squirmed at the touch and ducked under his arm.

"I am not. You're seeing things that aren't there." Selena managed to get to her desk and sit.

"That may be true but I'm feeling it, too. And between what I'm seeing and what I'm feeling, something's going on. If you're in trouble, you need to put it out on the table so I can help you." He paused for a moment and then turned and walked out the door leading to the housing units. Her tightly pressed lips must have given him the answer.

Conversation closed.

She should have just spilled it. DeNickey. Jeremy. Everything. Instead, she'd chosen not to call the cops, not to talk to Sam or call her father. Her hesitation *to do* anything was slowly closing the window of opportunity to do *anything* without casting suspicion her way. Why hadn't her father ever told her? Did he not trust her? And Jeremy. She'd fallen for their combative friendship, made it into something it was not. He was using her. She'd been too blind and stupid to see it for what it was. Could she protect her father from being deported if she worked with Jeremy to set up DeNickey?

~

After a fruitless day of pacing back and forth, trying to find answers, Selena walked into the gymnasium and heard the shouts of inmates before she saw them. Boxing night at the prison always fascinated her because many of the men were in for assaults and violent tempers and then encouraged to take up boxing. Of course, the program promoted control and discipline and only a handful of inmates were selected to train. The sport of boxing was a favorite of hers, too. Or had been until Jeremy's beating. Thug behavior, though, not boxing. The energy level in the building matched her own restless demeanor. She wished she could get in the ring and beat the daylights out of someone, gloves or no gloves.

Despite their earlier tension, Selena sat next to Sam, already waiting for the first event.

"Chaco's fighting." Sam mentioned an inmate they both knew.

"I heard. Thought I'd see if he was any good." Selena watched the other boxers.

Two bloody fights later, and Chaco was up. A young bi-racial kid with light-colored eyes, he had the enthusiasm and energy to make the main event. Dancing in from the boxer's corner, he focused on his opponent. His challenger was from the local boxing club, an outsider, which made the crowd roar louder for their guy.

The other boxer swayed on his feet, wiping blood on his glove as Chaco landed another leaden punch to his chin. The fight was declared over in minutes.

Chaco raised his hands high in victory. Jumping on the ropes, Chaco spurred the crowd in chants and cheers. He yelled out around his crimson-stained mouthpiece. "Hey, Ms. Maldanado! Did you see that?"

Selena rolled her eyes. Of all things…

Sam grinned at her. "Wow. Another admirer. You must feel proud."

"Shut up." Selena stood and made her way back through the throng of inmates to the upper gym floor, Sam close behind her. He gave her another once-over that nearly undid her and said goodbye.

Selena passed the room to the right of the gym and caught a glimpse of an older man and an inmate deep in conversation. The shaky writing on the blackboard caught her eye and she stepped into the room to see it clearer.

Truth is light.

Truth. Ugh. Not something she was knee-deep in at the moment. How do you feel about that, God? Surprised she was addressing an entity she had only approached in terms of "God is great, God is good", Selena stepped into the room. Both men raised their eyes to her.

"Sorry, didn't mean to bother you." Selena grabbed the nearest pamphlet and rushed out the door. Back at her office, she started to throw the paper away when she realized the same saying on the blackboard was also on the pamphlet.

This was Jolie "talk". Selena knew the terms, knew what truth and light meant, but together? They were obviously connected religiously. "Real and genuine" she understood. If she agreed to Jeremy's plan, neither of those would be true of her. Did she care? She was a good person essentially. And she'd be protecting her father.

<u>Truth and Light</u>

Truth is real and genuine, absence of darkness, unconcealed.

Light is spiritual enlightenment, the essence of reality.

The essence of reality made no sense. Her reality at the moment was pretty vague. The absence of darkness. Darkness was a part of her world as long as she worked at the prison and dealt with the ugliness of the place. Jolie was the brightest person in her life; her father, now a shadowy mixture of grey.

She would effectively destroy truth in her life if she followed through with Jeremy's plan. She would lose a piece of who she was if she went through with it. So where was God in all of this? Was He even real? If He was, like Rollos believed, she may need to get better acquainted. If He wasn't and the power was in her alone, like Jeremy said, she was in trouble.

Both Jeremy and DeNickey avoided her during the week. They'd apparently backed into their own corners, waiting for the storm to explode.

After much deliberation, Selena tried calling the ranch to talk with her father. If what Jeremy said wasn't true, then he had no leverage over her.

When she dialed the ranch, Jolie's response wasn't encouraging. She wouldn't elaborate and kept saying "You need to talk to him." Exasperated and unable to catch her father near a phone, Selena told Jolie she was coming home.

~

Selena sped down the highway, Patches slobbering in the front seat and a fresh Diet Coke in hand. Part of her wanted to walk right in and talk with her father, no hesitation; the other part wanted to delay the conversation. Maybe she didn't even want to know the truth. That word again, it seemed to haunt her.

After a brief pit stop at the side of the ranch house for the dog's benefit, Selena headed for the kitchen, Patches plodding along behind her. As she neared the central room of the house, she could hear voices and felt the old, familiar sounds melt her anxiety.

"Oh, you're home. Did you have a good trip?" Jolie hugged her.

"Yeah, but I'm a little anxious to talk to Papá."

"Sweetie, I know. He's out in the arena right now but he should be in any minute. Here, have some tea."

Ben, seated on a stool near where Jolie was making pastries, chimed in. "Hey, your dad has new horses in the barn. Tomorrow we can see how many times you can get bucked off one."

"No thanks." Selena didn't want to spend time bantering with Ben. Her heart was heavy and her emotions, grumpy. "I'm going to wait for Papá out on the porch. Come on, Patches."

A defiant Patches launched both paws on the counter and sideswiped a sugary donut hole.

"Get that dog out of my kitchen." Jolie clapped her hands at him. Selena backtracked and pulled a reluctant Patches out onto the porch.

She gazed out on the vista, rocking chair barely moving. A small breeze ruffled Patches' fur as he lay down next to her, a smidgen of sugar clinging to his chin. A pair of hummingbirds flitted in and out, in and out, drinking in the sweet nectar from the feeder. Selena watched as they dove and hovered, gaining the liquid with their tongues. Selena laid her head back and closed her eyes. There was nowhere as peaceful as home, and yet the turmoil raged inside her. So many unanswered questions. Why did she have to ask them, anyway? Couldn't everyone just leave well enough alone? A truck door slammed, bringing Selena up out of the chair.

"My beautiful girl, how was the drive?" Selena's Papá kissed both of her cheeks and then settled into the other rocker.

"It was fine." Silently, Selena contemplated which words to use first. Never before had talking to him been a problem. Now there was a barrier, an uncomfortable wall of too many thoughts not spoken.

"Papá-"

"Selena-" Both started at the same time. "Selena, I know you have questions. Let me tell you the story and then we can talk. Okay?"

"Okay." Selena rocked nervously. Her father had always been a truthful, hardworking, upstanding citizen. Had he really been keeping this from her?

"You know your mother died in childbirth with your younger brother. About the same time, Marco, my brother, got into really bad dealings with the police. He was finally caught outside of Mexico City hauling major amounts of marijuana in his truck. Because Marco was always over, eating dinner and jabbering about a job he didn't have, the police had him on record as being at our house a lot. Marco would never tell them who the dope was for or who was paying him, so they suspected his nearest relative. Me."

The scenario must have been devastating. In the midst of mourning the loss of his wife and son, the police showed up with more bad news.

"I took off with you. Making the matter worse, I'm sure." Manuel gazed out into the darkened yard.

"The whole thing is a sad story. I haven't spoken to Marco since we left town."

"Are there charges in Mexico for you?" Selena asked, dreading the answer.

"No. John checked before he let me stay on. They said there was nothing pending, and your padre wasn't a wanted man." Manual smiled. He patted her hand with his leathery, calloused one. "When I left, I took enough with me to care for you, the cornhusk doll your momma made that you loved, and started north."

Selena felt relief and sadness and pride well up in her. Pride for the way her father had protected her and made it far with a young girl in hand. Relief he wasn't involved in Marco's doings. How could anyone believe that about her father, anyway?

Sadness overwhelmed her. She'd never really known her mother or the baby who'd died. There weren't any pictures or keepsakes still in her possession. The little cornhusk doll, with its homemade clothing and carefully attached straw hair, was her only treasure from her mother. Her mother, as Papá told it, was beautiful in a clean, pure way. He always said Selena looked like her mother, with a smattering of freckles that came out if she stayed in the sun too long.

"Doing odd jobs for those who felt sorry for a father and his young daughter. I found those cattle and ran them up to Hidden Creek Ranch," he paused to wave a hand at the sign by the road boasting the ranch's brand, "and you know the rest of the story."

"You never got a green card?"

"What would I do with a green card? I wasn't

planning to go anywhere, John wasn't going to turn me in, you were settled." Manual wiped a handkerchief across his forehead. "Oh, me and John talked about it once but decided it was too much trouble. You know, hija, God has been good to us. I will never know why He took your momma and baby brother from us, but we made it safely here, and we have Jolie and John and many others that love and support both of us. God will continue to protect and guide us. I know this in my heart."

"So, you are illegal?" Selena felt her stomach rumble and the anxiety build again. Jeremy was right; her Papá was illegal.

"Illegal? If you want to call what I did illegal."

"Am I illegal?"

"No, hija. Your beautiful mother, God rest her soul, was a US citizen before moving to Mexico. You're legal."

Her father wasn't concerned about not having a green card. However, Jeremy might just pull some strings that could bring Marco back into the picture. And take her father down. Unless she did what he wanted. And her Papá's God? He could step in any time now.

28

During the ride home, Selena processed what she'd found out. Okay, her father was an illegal immigrant. Neither he nor the rancher seemed to care much. Tucked into their little niche of the world, a green card made no difference in their working relationship or daily lives. Jeremy, on the other hand, was forcing her hand, leading her to believe he had the ability to disrupt her father's well-being with one phone call to INS. If she didn't do what he wanted, Jeremy promised to make her life, and her family's, chaotic. If she did help him set DeNickey up, Jeremy said he'd leave everyone alone. Did she believe that? What about the others involved? Did they know about her? What if this was another string of lies and somehow, she got tangled in Jeremy's web? He could still call INS regardless of what she did.

Selena parked her vehicle on the driveway and let Patches run free onto the brick sidewalk around to the back. A partial foundation of a garage lined the far side with half walls made of cement enclosing three sides of the building. A pile of empty glass bottles lay at her feet. She picked one up and read its label in the glow of the yard light. IBC Root beer.

Grabbing it by the neck, she arched her arm over her head and flung it against the cement. As the bottle shattered, she felt knots in her shoulder disintegrate. She picked other bottles and catapulted them after the first. Slowly, the tension eased its hold on her shoulders and spine as she stretched and hurled the glass, watching the satisfactory explosions.

Round and round her thoughts went. Jeremy hates DeNickey. Why? Because he wants out and DeNickey won't let him as evidenced by the beating. How did she get in the middle of this? They had started out at odds with each other from day one of training, and it had progressively grown into a love/hate thing. Was DeNickey using her as leverage over Jeremy, to keep him in the game? That had to be it. And in return, Jeremy was using her to set up DeNickey.

Selena chucked another bottle at the wall.

Selena glanced at her phone. Twenty-seven messages. She flipped through caller ID, all from Jeremy. She checked the alarm set for morning and turned the phone on silent. She'd deal with him on another day.

~

Back in her car the next day, Selena yawned. No sleep at her house again. Breaking bottles usually helped with the stress, but her head wouldn't shut off. Selena stood in front of DeNickey's office for a scheduled meeting, her stomach turning over. Anything with this man was disgusting.

"Ah, my favorite gal has come for a visit." DeNickey said from his desk.

"No, just the Monday meeting." Selena cringed.

"Well, I don't have much to show you, except for this." DeNickey tossed her hometown paper across his desk. "I've been doing a little investigating of my own." The front-page article had a center picture of her on She'Daisy, racing through the arena, guns blazing. The picture was an old one, taken during one of the competitions.

Selena stared at the picture, willing herself to breathe normally. He was investigating her. And if he found the picture, he could find the arena…and her father.

And then *he* could call INS.

"Apparently there's more to you than I know." DeNickey grinned at her.

"You didn't know that I could shoot better than most of these men around here?" Attempting a bravado she didn't feel, Selena tried to steer him into less dangerous territory.

"Oh, I knew you could shoot. Your scores showed that. What I didn't realize was what a fine rider you are."

"I can ride."

"Apparently so."

"What's with the article? You're investigating me, now?"

"No, not really. Just looking around. Trying to see what Jeremy sees." A new threat hung in the air.

They were both using her.

"I'll keep up to date on this." DeNickey tapped the photo. "Since my favorite gal doesn't tell me things." He winked at her.

Selena walked out, wishing for a shower.

What if she worked late tonight and after

everyone left the building, she just looked at the marijuana in the confiscation room? Not everyone had a key, but she knew where DeNickey kept his, which meant she'd have to break into his office. Or she could ask Sam, he had connections. But that might bring up questions. She'd be better off leaving Sam out of it. The fewer involved, the better. She was really going to do this?

At an hour past shift change, Selena made her way upstairs to see who was still around. Just the guards at the airlocks. She was glad she wouldn't be bringing anything in or out of the prison but rather shifting its place on the inside. A half-asleep guard let her back through the control center and down into the stairwell to her office.

Pausing by DeNickey's door, Selena took a deep breath and tried her office key in the lock. Click. Selena stepped into the darkened office, expecting the deep voice of DeNickey to jump from the shadows. Nothing greeted her, but silence. Softly closing the door behind her, Selena locked it and flipped on the lights. The key was usually in his desk drawer and when she pulled on it, the entire contents nearly fell to the floor. Used toothpicks, snotty rags, and scribbled notes greeted her. Selena grabbed a pen from the holder on the desk and reached for the key ring. Small locker keys and obvious door keys were attached to a key ring that said "Gentleman's Ranch" in neon colors. More grossness.

Selena put the key ring in her pocket and backed out of the room. Coast still clear. Her first illegal act, breaking into DeNickey's office and desk. Selena thought about her father. This was all really for him.

She didn't want him deported due to an ancient decision that had, in the end, seemed justified and responsible. Or be used by these two men.

Plagued with doubts, Selena walked around the corner and through the Orientation room to where they kept confiscated items. The cavernous room held a multitude of things, picked off of inmates entering the prison. It also held prohibited inventory found during cell searches and illegal contraband gathered from visitors. Tall, storage lockers labeled Weapons, Drugs, Items to be Returned, Police Cases stood against one wall. A wooden table sat in the center of the room, large enough for a small class to attend brief, informative meetings about confiscated items from the previous shifts. Chain-of-command sheets and other necessary paperwork and baggies were stuffed in drawers under the cubby holes at the entrance to the room. Plastic gloves filled a Kleenex box in one of the holes.

Selena stretched plastic gloves on her sweaty hands and muttered to herself. She'd reduced herself to a common criminal. She was no better than they were. Selena thought again about her father. All this time, he had protected her, brought her to a safe place, landed a good job that he loved, and had confidently placed his trust in God, a being she had never fully understood. She wanted to do everything in her power to protect him now. Forget God. She would be the one taking care of him, repaying her father for all of the wonderful years he had given her.

Selena looked at the keys she'd picked up from DeNickey's desk. One of the smaller gold ones probably fit the locker labeled Drugs. Technically, the marijuana should have been moved from the Drugs cabinet to the Police Case cabinet and turned over to the DEA's office almost immediately, according to Jeremy.

Successful with her first attempt, the lock released its grip. The upper shelf held various pipes and paraphernalia; the second shelf was full of tiny baggies of pills with several glass containers of liquids. Selena had seen the hooch inmates made in their rooms with fruit, a required food item by the state legislatures, and sugar packets. It smelled nasty, looked worse, and could send a heavy-set man into alcoholic seizures quickly if left to ferment for too long.

She carefully looked at the baggies of marijuana. Selena hung her head and leaned against the locker. *I have to do this.* The thought made her nauseous. Jeremy's beaten and bruised face came to mind. DeNickey wouldn't stop. Not until he'd done all the damage he wanted to do. Jeremy wouldn't either, until he was clear of DeNickey. A migraine brewed right behind her eyes.

Selena took a bag out of the locker and placed it on the table. She reached for a smaller baggie. If she was going to plant this, she'd have to transfer it a third time to some Saran Wrap since the inmates didn't have access to Confiscation baggies. Selena scoffed. She made a really bad criminal.

As she opened the bag, the rancid smell of marijuana rose. It's musty, grassy-sweet odor spread through the room. Selena sealed the contents and stuffed it into her pocket. Returning the bigger baggie to its original place, Selena left the

Confiscation room as it had been before she'd crept in.

After returning the keys to DeNickey's desk and locking his office door, Selena turned to find a Control center guard standing next to her.

He assessed her with his eyes. "What are you doing?"

29

Brandon watched the inmates line up around the basketball court. Without a net, a device the guards thought the convicts could live without, the basketball silently slid through the hoop, hitting the cement with a muffled thwack. Absent-mindedly, he scratched his tattoo, a reminder of the group he belonged to. It was a far cry from the ones portrayed on any of the guys in front of him. His had three crosses on a mountaintop, the center one elevated slightly.

He stood a few paces away, separated from the crowd, trying to assess the source of his anxiety. For days now, he'd felt an oncoming train of destruction plowing through the inmates. There were always grumbling, complaining men roaming the yard, but this felt different, evil.

Brandon started to circle around the crowd, watching the players choose teams in typical prison lingo.

"We want the girl in the pretty shirt over there."

"This is my boy."

"We're bringing it."

A friendly game of basketball in prison could quickly escalate into a mad dog fight, but Brandon didn't sense any tension among the players.

Was it in him? The tension was in him? He headed toward the gym, hoping Mr. Trichler might be there. Maybe a visit from Suzie would help him relax and see a bigger picture.

A knot of men broke off their conversation as he passed them. Brandon was careful not to look any of them in the eye. He stepped into the small classroom that served as a semi-private chapel and sat in one of the metal chairs across from the row of windows that allowed guards to see into the room.

The last time he'd been here, Mr. Trichler talked to him about truth and light and how truth could set a person free. Free was a term not easily identified in a place like this. Emotional freedom came in knowing the truth that someone bigger than himself was watching over him and that he wasn't alone. Brandon picked up a Bible someone had left from the last service.

The scripture Mr. Trichler had shown him was in Romans. "And we know that all things work together for good for those that love God and are called to His purpose." A promise. Also not a term generally used in prison. Whatever God had called him to do, God would be faithful to cause it to turn for good. He was afraid, a gut feeling, that things were about to turn ugly. Good was promised in the end, though, according to the scriptures. Brandon breathed deeply. Whatever was in the air, or in him, causing the anxiety would be revealed. For now, sleep was his best plan. Deep, thoughtless sleep.

~

Jeremy dabbed at the cut above his eye. It had broken open again, causing blood to drip onto his cheek. A pretty good gash. The rest of his body ached worse, aspirin barely able to dull the pain.

Where was Selena? He'd tried calling her ten times in the last half hour. She wasn't answering her pager or her cell phone.

DeNickey was hot about Jeremy wanting out of the game and for mentioning the marijuana that someone else had brought in. None of it was worth it anymore. His sister wasn't getting better, her bills were still mounting despite Jeremy's desperate actions to cover them, and Selena, well, Selena didn't understand. He really hated how he'd involved her. He should never have pursued her, especially with DeNickey in the picture. A smart, beautiful woman in his career field who was on the opposite side of the law than he was at the moment, Selena would have been a perfect match for him if he hadn't had to jeopardize everything for DeNickey.

Did she go back to the ranch? Was she out with someone else? That guy she worked with, Sam? Maybe she went to the bar where some of her co-workers hung out.

Jeremy pulled on his coat. He was going to find her. She had to come through for him. Even if he would have chosen not to involve her, she was already there.

~

Selena entered the bar and sat far from the sweaty man most of the waitresses were avoiding.

The bartender hollered at him to lay off the girls or he'd find himself out the door. The man snickered and dropped his gaze back into the bottom of his glass.

"Hey, what can I get you?" the barkeep asked her.

After a long hesitation, Selena muttered. "Thanks, but nothing. This was a mistake." She thought a drink would help calm her nerves after being caught in the hallway, fist clenched around the baggie in her pocket. The officer had teased her about working too hard, made some passing shoot-the-breeze comments, and moved on down the hall. She'd scurried back to her office, stashed the drugs under a file drawer, grabbed her windbreaker, and walked out of the prison as nonchalantly as possible.

Now, sleep was beginning to overtake her body, the anxiety settling behind her shoulder blades. She just needed to go to bed.

Selena found her way through the pulsating bodies to the fresh air outside. Pulling keys out of her pocket, she ran into someone coming into the bar.

"Sorry." She started. "Jeremy. What are you doing?" She glanced around as if the cops would already be swarming around her

"I could ask you that. I've been calling for hours. Where have you been?"

Jeremy's face looked stormy with his puffy eyes and crusty blood over the worst of the gashes.

"Where have I been?" Selena echoed.

Jeremy grabbed her arm, tightening his grip. "I said I've been calling for hours."

"Are you serious? Let go of me."

Jeremy released his grip on her. "Look, I'm sorry. This whole thing is getting to me. I couldn't reach you after I dropped that load on you about your father."

"You're stalking me."

"I am not stalking you."

"Oh, really? How many times did you call my phone tonight? Ten? Twenty? And what about the time you just happened to be in the neighborhood? Or the time you were sitting out front of my house, just waiting for me to come home? Or the biggest of all, when you followed me to the ranch? Why? Because you are stalking me."

"I am not. I am trying to help, to protect you. You know what, though? If you won't help me, I can't help you." Jeremy strode away from her.

Selena watched him, apprehension squeezing the breath from her.

"Jeremy, wait." Selena called after him, her voice drowning in the revving of his motorcycle. Jeremy gunned the engine and pulled alongside her open door.

"What?"

"This thing, DeNickey, you, it's giving me nightmares. It's over my head."

"I think we both are." Jeremy shut the bike off. "If we take out DeNickey, we're both free. You're free of me. I'm free of him. I'll find another way to help my sister."

Wiping the back of her hand across her face, Selena slumped in the seat. She wanted to trust him, but she didn't. This was all too overwhelming, a jigsaw puzzle with pieces all alike.

Uncomprehendingly difficult and impossible to figure out.

"I moved the stuff."

30

Sam stuck his head in the door of her office as Selena popped the top on her morning's second can of Coke.

"What? A two-coke day again?" he nodded at the cans on her desk.

"Yeah. Did you need something or can I get back to work now?" Edgy from the late night talking with Jeremy and the knowledge Sam was inches away from where she'd hidden the stash of marijuana, Selena dissuaded him from entering her office.

"Wow, you're grumpy today."

"What a nice thing to say." Selena turned to her computer, facing away from Sam. He started to back out just as DeNickey stepped in.

"Wait, Sam, we weren't finished with our conversation." She turned back around, desperately not wanting to be alone in the room with DeNickey. Had the officer told him about last night, finding her outside his office?

Holding Sam's eyes, she silently pleaded with him to stay. Sam came to a military-at-ease. Sam, her loyal friend, wasn't going anywhere.

"I'll be out of the prison for a few days while I catch up on some business, if you know what I mean." DeNickey winked at Sam. "Maldanado, I put you as lead investigator while I'm gone. Don't screw it up. Sam, I wish you were on my team. I'd put you as lead. Why I have to put a girl in charge is beyond me." DeNickey muttered on the way out the door.

Sam stood quietly, tight-lipped. "So, do you really want to finish our conversation?"

"Yes… no. I didn't want to be in the room with him alone." Selena peeled the skin around her cuticles.

"There is no more conversation?"

"No."

"Selena, what is happening? Suddenly we're not good enough friends for you to tell me? If it's DeNickey, I'll help you. We all know he's a loser. If it's Jeremy, I'll listen. Can't say I like the guy much, but you seem to."

Selena looked up at him, scanning his face. She knew Sam cared about her, knew she was more than a mentee to him. Here he stood, offering his help and he had no idea how in over her head she was in mud and manure and slime. She couldn't talk to him about DeNickey and what she'd taken from the Confiscation room. She obviously couldn't tell him about Jeremy. It was pointless to say anything at all.

"Really, I'm okay. My migraines have come back, and I can't shake them without a load of caffeine." It was the easiest resolution to the conversation and true.

"And grumpiness."

"What? Oh, yeah, and with a load of

grumpiness. Sorry." Selena smiled back at him and watched as Sam walked back to his office.

As she checked the doorway for any more unwanted visitors, her eyes slid to where the marijuana was. She opened the file drawer and felt for the stash taped to the underside. She let out her breath. It was still there, but the faint smell of marijuana permeated the drawer. She'd have to move it soon, or her whole office would reek.

~

Brandon headed out to the yard for some quieter air. The inside of the housing unit was always loud with inmates clanging doors or yelling to each other. He wished he had a headset with a riff of blues playing in his ears.

Seeing Maldanado walk across the yard, he decided to follow her and see what she was doing this morning. With her wind-whipped hair loosely braided down her back, she looked like a fresh-faced college kid trying to act grown-up. Most of the inmates ignored her until she passed them, but a few were brazen enough to catcall. Brandon shook his head. Bigger and tougher men had been chewed up and spit out as garbage in the prison setting.

Still, Maldanado seemed to be holding her own. He watched as she stopped and talked to several inmates. Her curves were barely concealed under her loose-fitting clothing, and he knew he wasn't the only one who snagged a glimpse. He'd seen both inmates and guards look if only for the briefest of seconds.

Brandon sauntered over to the fence near her. Like most inmates, complaining was the name of the game. This one centered on the food service.

"Now, you know, ma'am, what these here friends of mine are going through? You don't eat in the cafeteria, do ya?" The inmate with the scraggly beard became the orator of the group.

"No, I don't." Selena shook her head.

"Ma'am, that food ain't fit for a broken-down sow to eat." He continued complaining.

"Have you filed a grievance with Mr. DeNickey?" Selena asked.

The other inmates snorted. The talker of the group shuffled his feet and searched the ground.

"How long you been at this prison?" he said, scratching himself. "Not long at'all, I'm suspecting. 'Cause if you'd had, you'd know DeNickey ain't caring one way t'the other what happens down here. Unless someone gets theselves kilt. Or is participatin' any e-legal activities."

Brandon watched the others around her nod in agreement.

"Mr. DeNickey isn't much help to you?"

"Ha. What rock did you crawl out from?" One of the men spoke up and then spat a line of tobacco behind her. Brandon watched, but she didn't flinch. "Or crib I should say?"

Brandon wanted to reach out and remind the man of his manners, but he chose instead to look the other direction.

Selena did not respond to the jeer and continued to listen intently to the inmates' complaints.

"He'd better watch out, though. There's a bunch of us who's just about tired of being ignored. We's about to have a time of it."

Selena left without hearing the parting words of the ringleader.

"Ain't she right perty? If'n we did have us a situation, I might take it in my head to keep her with me for a bit."

Brandon shuddered. That man would be one to keep an eye out for, but honestly, many of the inmates probably thought the same way. If anything did break out, she'd be a prime target. Surely, they wouldn't let her down on the yard if the tension rose any higher. Only God would be able to protect her if they did.

~

Selena moved back toward her office. Things were so complicated she was having difficulty keeping her ducks in a row. Driving home last night, she'd passed the interstate that ran from one coast to the other. All the way, she'd thought about how it would be if she could just turn left or right onto the interstate and drive until she couldn't drive anymore. Of course, she'd miss Patches, her constant car companion. The interstate might be a temporary solution to the fog in her head, but it wouldn't last long. Now if she could get on a horse and ride like the wind for a couple of hours, that'd be a great temporary solution, too.

"Hello?" Selena picked up her office phone on the first ring.

"Hey. How's today shaping up for you?" Jeremy's voice grated on her nerves.

"It's a tough day. I can't really talk."

"I won't keep you." Jeremy paused. "You will tell me when your end is complete, won't you? It would be difficult for me to do my end if you don't."

"I know. I'll let you know. Please don't push me." Selena glanced at the drawer with its hidden stash.

"I'm not. I want to know what's going on." Jeremy whined. "I'm sorry. These cuts are starting to heal, and they itch, and I'm wound up about everything. The sooner it's over, the less I have to look over my shoulder. Sorry."

Selena felt the frustration in his voice; it mimicked her own.

"Listen, Jeremy, I've got to go."

"Okay. I'll see ya tonight."

"No, I won't be there." But he had already hung up.

31

Selena lifted the tape off the baggie of marijuana and glanced for the tenth time out the window. Nobody was around. Stuffing the small amount into a wrapper used by the inmates to roll cigarettes, she pushed it deep inside her satchel and left the office.

The first name that came to mind for the receiver of the marijuana, was the snotty inmate, Watson that had eaten the paper with her name on it.

She watched for him before entering the control area. Look normal. A normal afternoon. Doing what she would normally do. Yeah, right. Setting up an inmate and the investigator all in a normal day's work. Grabbing a tissue, she sponged her face free of the sweat on her brow and upper lip.

"Afternoon." The control room officer said, glancing over his shoulder. Intent on watching a cell in the far wing, he continued. "A little tattooing going on somewhere, and they think the ink is being melted down in one of our showers." The guard snorted.

Selena pasted a smile on her face. If he only knew what her plans were. "I hear there's a little more than that going on."

"Not in my house." The guard grimaced.

"Can I look at your cell roster?" Selena gripped her satchel tighter.

"Sure, who you lookin' for?"

"Nobody in particular. Just placin' everybody in case I need to know." Normal procedure to know where troublesome inmates reside. Normal. "This guy's Mexican Mafia, right?" She pointed to a known gang member. Pick out a few names, throw the scent off.

"Yeah, but he's small potatoes. He answers to Sorrento over in Housing Unit #4."

"Ah, and Bastilla?"

"He claims Mafia, but I doubt it. I don't see no markings on him." The guard referred to the MM brand.

"What about Pratt?"

"Nasty dude. Always covered in baby powder."

She continued down the list, slightly pausing next to Watson. Noting the cell number, she asked a few more questions and then gave the roster back.

"Hey, I'm going to use your restroom and then walk the pod and see what I can see." Selena swung her satchel over her shoulder and headed to the staff bathroom near the caseworker's offices.

"They'll all be unlocked unless someone is..." the guard made an unpleasant remark about the inmate's elimination process.

Selena closed the door to the staff-only bathroom. She turned around in the small, cramped area and pulled the marijuana from her satchel. Staring at the illegal substance, she thought about her options. She wasn't so deep she couldn't get out yet. She could flush the marijuana and be done with it, conscious cleared. Selena held the baggie over the lid-less toilet. *Just drop it.* It would take seconds to dissolve the wrapper and flush the offending mess out into the sewage pit. *Just drop it.*

No. She'd come this far. She was here, the time was now. Selena pushed the cigarette behind her corrections badge and left the restroom.

She stepped into the wing and listened for sounds of activity. Noticing which cells were open and emanating voices, she kept an eye on incoming traffic. If she saw Watson come in, the plan would be aborted.

Act normal.

Selena touched the pouch behind her badge where she'd hidden the marijuana. Using her prison ID badge for the stash was ironic. Everything she'd worked for, proving herself over and over again, was tied up in what that badge meant to her. DeNickey would have hired her on the spot for looks alone, but she'd satisfactorily navigated all of the tests and the warden's hiring board. Her badge was the accumulation of all the things she'd dreamt of. Now here she was using the very token of her hard work to execute a crime.

Selena chanced a look at the bubble area in the center of the four wings. They weren't paying attention to her. She stopped and took a deep breath. Watson's cell was to the left of her. Opportunity rose like a dragon. Breathing a frothy mixture of guilt and anxiety, she struggled to look beyond to Jeremy's bruised and battered face, to her father's unpretentious one. She had to do this. It was now or never.

Selena walked into Watson's domain and noted the pin-up girls on one side of the room. His apparently religious cellmate's poster on the other wall, said "Live Free". She felt divided as if she were walking a tightrope between them. How could an inmate live free? She wasn't in prison and couldn't seem to live free; free from the burden of responsibility, free from the onslaught of guilt, her own imposed jail.

Standing in the room, she still had the option to walk away. She could leave it all alone and let the pieces fall as they may, or she could trip the trigger bringing down DeNickey and his incessant pursuit of Jeremy. A pursuit that would likely land her father back in Mexico if circumstances didn't work out.

Knowing time was short, she scanned the bunks for a place to plant the drugs. It didn't even matter which bunk she planted it on. The motion was set, and she couldn't undo her actions once she dropped the drugs. Looking under the top bunk near the welding marks of the metal frame, she caught a glimpse of a sharpened profile. Watson felt the need for a little protection, did he?

Selena retrieved the rolled-up marijuana from behind her badge and stuck it up by the honed pen casing. Now what? Should she tell the captain on shift about the hidden shank? Coupled with the sit-down discussions rumored throughout the prison, it might be the instigator she needed.

Moving quickly out of the cell, Selena visited three other cells before returning to the control area for her satchel.

"Find anything of the domino-burners?" asked the guard.

Selena shook her head. "No. But I can tell you, word's still out about a sit-down."

The guard grunted. "They're always threatening a sit-down. Never seems to matter over what."

"Well, I didn't see any evidence of tatting going on."

"I knew we didn't have 'em in our house."

Selena didn't mention she hadn't visited every room or that the house may be invaded shortly by the black-clad E-Squad. Much bigger things were going to hit the fan than a little tattoo business. Fearful of saying too much, she left the housing unit. She'd done it, set the bait. There wasn't any way to take it back now. She had to ride the bull the whole eight seconds and hope she didn't get skewered in the process.

On the sidewalk, she encountered Sam's clerk. He nodded to her and made his way into the building.

32

Brandon watched Maldanado brush past him without acknowledgment. Maldanado had been in the field long enough to get her feet wet. Brandon wondered when she would get burned or burned out as so many did. She was heading down a bad fork in the road. Maybe Sam was her grounding. Or her protector. Anyway, if Suzie thought something was up with her, it probably was, and it'd bode well for none of them.

As Brandon entered the housing unit and briefly met eyes with the control area officer, a kid from across the wing hollered at him. The kid was young, but his cellmate was an old time con, not usually a good combination. For the moment, the old con was taking a defensive role with him, protecting him from the predators. Brandon heard from the old timer the kid occasionally cried himself to sleep. Luckily, the old man didn't speak to many and only let it slip to Brandon.

"Mike." Brandon addressed him.

"That lady investigator was in your cell. She come down to talk and went through several 'em. You got anything in there?" Mike shifted from foot to foot.

Brandon blanched.

"Did she take anything out?" He let out a long breath.

"Nope, not out of yours. I didn't see her take nothing out of nobody's."

"Thanks for telling me. Want me to teach you chess tonight so you can play Gordy?" Brandon distracted Mike from following him to the cell.

"Yeah." A big smile lit up Mike's face. It was hard not to call him "Mikey" when he looked like that.

Leaving Mike at the picnic table, Brandon slowly entered his cell. At first glance, nothing seemed amiss. If she had found anything, especially her own picture, the e-squad would have rained down on him in a hurry. Hopping up on the top bunk, he looked at a slight tear in the plastic cover and checked his hiding spot. It didn't look invaded. He ran his fingers along the side of the mattress.

Everything was as he had left it.

Sirens sounded from outside the housing unit. Large outdoor speakers sputtered to life. "ATTENTION. ATTENTION ALL HOUSING UNITS. All inmates must report back to their cells immediately"

Inmates flooded the wing as Brandon watched from his cell door. Sweat began to roll down his back.

If they were locking down the prison, he'd be stuck with Maldanado's stuff in his room for good. If they were searching for something in particular, there'd be no way his room would go unsearched.

Panic caught in his throat. This may be the end of what he'd been working for. If they found it, he'd go directly to Administrative Segregation and probably be shipped out to another facility before he could even get a phone call in to Suzie. God be with them.

"Hey, Gordy. You know what this is about?" Brandon paused in front of Mike and Gordy's cell, using the movement of the other inmates in the housing unit to disappear inside.

"Nope. Not routine, though." Gordy pulled on his scraggly beard.

Brandon slid back over to his cell as Watson joined him at the door.

"What's all this?" his cellmate asked.

"Don't know." Brandon wrinkled his nose at his cellmate's odor. The man always smelled. Brandon couldn't pinpoint when the guy had taken a shower last. He glanced back at the bunk where Maldanado's pic was. If they found it, he could spin a story of some sort. Maybe tell the guards she'd given it to him. As a what, gift? Pay-off? Would they believe that? It would ruin her career if she were caught being friendly with an inmate. And effectively shut down her involvement with the drug activity. They might not believe his story, but it would certainly throw suspicion her way.

Brandon and his cellmate stood outside their cell and waited for the impromptu count to complete. From the looks of Gordy's room, they were tearing up the cells on their way through. Whatever had alerted the guards must have been big. A little threat of a sit-down wouldn't have provoked this type of response.

He watched as the emergency squad bagged up contraband from the various rooms. He knew from conversations overheard in Sam's presence all of it would be processed through the investigator's office.

Maldanado. Why did everything point back to her? Trouble seemed to follow her. She had been in his cell. Mike said she'd been in a lot of them. But if she'd found the picture, the e-squad would have only descended on his cell and not the whole prison. Why didn't she take it? Why let E-squad tear everyone's cell up? Maybe they didn't know what they were looking for? Maybe it was a blanket search.

~

Sam watched as inmates were brought down to his housing unit. If he'd known a mass search was scheduled for today, he could have brought in additional staff. Or at least, stocked up on Coke. Maybe Selena could help. Where she was in this headache? Probably had her own mess, sorting out the contraband heading her way. Of all the times for DeNickey to be off with…. Sam couldn't even finish the sentence so wide were the possibilities.

Sam's officers scurried from the white board where each name was added to cells as they transported inmates. Those found with serious contraband, shanks, drugs, and threatening letters landed themselves in Administrative Segregation. Crude posters or kites, letters passed between inmates, went with just a slap and a written violation. A disciplinary hearing would be scheduled later.

Officers checked in with him as they handed off paperwork. Angry retorts, sweat dripping from officers' caps, and the rising humidity invading the air-conditioned office each time a new transfer arrived put Sam's teeth on edge. He struggled to control his temper as he thought of whoever had launched this prison-wide search. He was easily accessible; he could have been forewarned. Instead, they had left him in the lurch, cleaning up the mess.

Selena arrived, pale and scattered, as Sam was locking another inmate into his new temporary home. He was very aware of the filthy words being tossed at officers like grenades and violence close to the surface. Despite his revulsion of mankind at the moment, he could really use her help.

Let her help.

"Hey," Selena handed him more paperwork.

"Hey." Sam unlocked the cuffs of the newest resident through the feed door and closed it with a slam. Looking at Selena more directly, she seemed upset. Maybe she had one of her migraines. He knew he was certainly brewing one. "You know what this is all about?"

"Sort of. After talking with several inmates, the sit-down was imminent."

"We don't usually lock down the prison on a possibility."

"Well, I, I mentioned it to the captain, and he thought a shake down might prevent it." Selena worked a torn cuticle to a bloody, raw spot.

"Or start it. A shake down is one thing, but look around you. This is chaos."

"I didn't order it. Don't yell at me." Selena pulled herself up to his height.

"Okay, okay, I won't yell. I just don't understand it. This will take weeks to work out." Sam ran his hands through his cropped hair. Beaded sweat broke out on his temples.

"I know. I'll help you. For a Diet Coke." Selena attempted to coax a smile from him.

As they were handing off the cuffs to the control area officer, another group of inmates were brought down the walk. Among them, Watson stood out with his braids stuck straight up in the air. Right behind him, eyes to the ground, Sam's clerk stutter-stepped in front of the transporting guard.

~

"What the?" Selena heard Sam say beside her.

Selena felt only a small bit of satisfaction when she saw Watson in the mix. The plan was working, but it was causing a lot of hard work on Sam's part. Selena sucked in her breath when she realized Sam's clerk was also in the group. What was he doing there? Had Sam misjudged his clerk? He'd acted like a decent guy for someone locked up. Not innocent, just decent. He'd been loyal to Sam, respectful to Selena, even protecting her to a degree from the yard violence.

Selena saw Sam and his clerk catch eyes. Sam's narrowed as he broke contact with him. Putting an arm out, he stopped the transporting officer.

"What'd he do?" Sam's voice sounded hoarse.

Brandon stopped with the officer and lifting his eyes, stared straight at Selena. She almost took a step back.

"Found pot in his cell. And some other things." The officer's clipped tone told of his own long day. Glancing at Selena, he asked Sam if he could talk with him later.

"Yep, get him settled in and come find me." Sam didn't even look at the inmate who he had marginally trusted as his clerk.

Selena felt her head turn into a bundle of pulsating nerves. Bright, tiny flashes of light in her peripheral vision signaled the growing migraine. This was a nightmare.

Was the pot found in Sam's clerk's bunk what she had planted? She hadn't even looked at Watson's cellmate's name. Was it possible he was Sam's clerk?

Selena blew out another breath and tried to loosen the tightening noose in her chest. She reminded herself it didn't really matter who got caught with the dope as long as it was put out there and could be traced back to DeNickey. She'd have to do step two and tell the authorities she suspected DeNickey or let Jeremy step in and explain. Which he wouldn't do. Had she thought this through? Was she sinking her own ship? The dream of being a hotshot investigator was quickly dissipating, and she felt the chains to that dream tighten.

Selena snorted. Didn't really matter. She had started the process and now ruined another relationship, the one between Sam and his clerk. She'd never consciously do something to cause grief to Sam. Or his clerk. Rollos had been nothing but appropriate towards her. Even kind if she was being honest. He was about to be collateral damage.

Sam hung his head after his now-ex clerk passed him. Selena stood still, wanting to reassure him somehow, but unable to give away her own involvement.

"I wish I smoked." Sam pushed his hands in his pockets.

Turning back into the building, Selena followed him to his office. They sat in silence, filling out segregation forms for each of the inmates brought in.

"Sir?" Sam and Selena looked up at the officer in the doorway. "I checked Rollos in."

"Yeah, I saw."

Selena turned back to the paperwork. Part of the plan was done. Let the pieces fall where they may.

The officer glanced from Sam to Selena and back to Sam.

"She's an investigator. Nothing you say in here won't get back to her. You're free to talk." Sam reassured him.

"Well, sir, the other stuff we found in Rollos' cell…well, it's a picture of Maldanado."

"WHAT?" Sam stood.

Selena glanced at the officer as she felt her vision cloud.

33

"What do you mean a picture of Maldanado?" Sam slammed his fist down on the desk.

Selena closed her eyes. What picture? Where did he get it? When? The room began to spin, and her vision continued to cloud. She had inadvertently set up Sam's clerk to take the fall to ruin DeNickey, but in the meantime he had a picture of her in his cell? Why? Was she being set up? Again?

The guard cursed. "It's in a little frame. A picture of Maldanado and a horse," the guard paused, embarrassed.

Sam's face was ashen.

A horse? Like as in She'Daisy? A picture from her office?

The guard hooked his thumbs in his pockets.

Selena looked from Sam to the guard. This was bad.

Sam turned away from the guard and toward her. "Do you know how he could have gotten this?"

"Don't you mean, did I give it to him?" Selena's vision skittered again to the guard. They had to settle this now in front of the guard. If they didn't, he'd spread his story around.

"No, that's not what I asked." Sam's voice was hard. Too hard. She knew he was pushed to the brink.

"Just so we're clear, I didn't give the picture to him." Selena stood facing Sam, her voice matching his.

The guard looked at the floor.

"That's still not what I asked."

Selena felt her insides wither. Sam had never spoken to her that way. "I don't know."

"Somehow, he got it. Who else knows what you picked up?" Sam looked at the guard.

"No one, sir. I knew you were friends, well, I knew," the guard cursed again in frustration. "I knew Maldanado, sir."

Neither man looked at her.

"I wanted to talk to you before I had to fill out the paperwork. He'll get written up for the pot, but whether or not the other thing gets in the report..." the guard risked a glance at her. She continued her silence.

"Well, we know she wasn't in on it. He picked it up somehow." Anger tightened Sam's voice.

"Sir, I can get rid of the pic if you want. Nobody has to know." The guard tapped the cigarettes in his pocket. "I can also, sir, take care of the inmate, sir, if you want." The young man pulled a cigarette out and fingered it, rubbing it between his palms, releasing the tobacco smell into the office.

Was he suggesting they transfer the inmate to another facility? Ignore the pot charge and release him back to general population with a snitch tag? Or take care of him like in the old mafia movies? As in dead, disappeared, no longer a threat? Selena's stomach turned.

"Let's not complicate this. Let me think on it." Sam slid into his chair. He absently scratched the Navy tattoo on his forearm. "Bruce, leave it here and I'll let you know in the next hour."

Pushing stuff out of his pocket, the officer laid the picture on Sam's desk. "I stuffed it in my pocket."

It was a picture of herself and She'Daisy.

"Thanks." Sam waited until the guard had left and then raised tired eyes to her.

"Why would he have this?" Selena tried to keep the quake from her voice.

"I don't know. And I don't know what to do about it." Sam stood and shut the glass door to his office. "I have to ask. You really don't know how he got it? DeNickey didn't set you up? Someone else hasn't got a beef with you? Jeremy?" Sam spit the words out.

Selena sat for a minute to compose an answer. She felt guilty, dirty, traitorous, even though she hadn't had anything to do with the clerk having her stuff. Her feelings about the dope and DeNickey and Jeremy were overlapping each other. The migraine was nearly incapacitating.

"No, nothing. I can't think of anything."

Thunder broke through the crackly air sending sweaty hairs to a standing position on her neck.

"Great. A storm. Fits the mood."

Thunder echoed through the housing unit as rain pelted the tin roof.

He took things out of her office or were they given to him? And he was going to do what with them? Show the other inmates? Blackmail her?

Never mind his cell was where she planted the drugs. Maybe it was God watching out for her. Maybe he led her to that cell knowing the clerk had things set up in his own court.

Selena winced at the thought. There was no way God was involved in this. If He was, it wasn't very humorous and actually pretty spiteful. No. She'd planted the drugs for her father's sake. She'd had to finagle the circumstances a little, but the end result was what counted, right? First, she had to get this thing with the clerk settled and then she'd push the plan through regardless of who got stung by it. She'd smooth it out with Sam and put it all behind her.

"Sam, look. DeNickey's gone, and there are others who could handle this, but just let me talk to Rollos. Maybe he'll give me something, so I'll know where and how he got the picture. I know it's the one from the shelf in my office." She could feel the humidity rising as the storm blew in. How dare he ruin her plans? She couldn't let this interfere; she had to make him talk.

"NO." Guards looked in from the glass windows. Sam waved them away. "Do you know how much trouble he's in? It's beyond a layer of crap sticking to the bottom of his boots; it's way up around his neck. Do you think I'm going to let you waltz in there and chat with him? I'll take care of it myself. And if what I have to say doesn't get him, well, I just may let Bruce at him."

Selena held her throbbing head. "Sam, listen to me. I can go in there and trap him into saying just about anything. Maybe I can convince him I'm on his side. You're not going to get anything out of him acting like a raging bull."

Sam sat, uncrossed his arms and leaned as far back in his chair as possible. "How did this day get so bad?"

Selena looked up when a loud thunderclap rumbled across the building.

"Come on, please? Let me have a go at him. If it doesn't work, I'll talk to Bruce myself. You can put him in with Bubba down the hall if you want." Selena choked out a dry laugh.

"DeNickey will kill me. This is totally out of procedure."

"What if he's involved? And when have we ever worked totally by the book? Half the time, we make it up as we go along."

"Yeah, but this is you and me. I don't want to bury our butts in some kind of stupid plan of DeNickey's."

"You know he'll bury my butt anyway when he gets back. He takes every opportunity."

Sam looked up at the tone of her voice.

"Are you sure DeNickey's not involved? Harassing you? Setting you up?" Sam asked.

Selena rubbed her hands on her jeans. He was so close.

"He always harasses me, you know that."

"Yeah, but maybe it's gotten worse than you're admitting. Trying to handle it on your own."

Selena kept her mouth closed. Sam looked at her for a long painful minute.

"Here's the problem with your plan. I left Brandon in your office for half a second while I grabbed some files. I thought he was in eyesight the whole time, but apparently not. I'm sorry. This is my fault. I'll talk to him, or we can go together. I have some choice words for him myself."

"Oh, Sam. Why did you need to unlock my office? Why not leave him standing with you in Orientation?" Selena covered her eyes with her elbow and put her head down on the table. Sam had just made everything worse and didn't even realize it.

"I needed the keys to the locker in Orientation, alright? I've got to check the weather with the control officers, Stay here. Please. Until I get back." Sam walked to the door. "We'll go talk to him, see what we can find out. If you aren't getting anything, I'll handle it from there. No sense you getting in too deep on this one, especially if it was my fault."

Too deep? Too late.

34

Without waiting for Sam, Selena made her way to the cell block. Far before she hit the door, she could hear the loud, angry voices of the inmates locked up "for no good reason," as well as their vulgar language.

Selena entered the Administrative Segregation area. Only one other person, a guard, was with her, and he was busy stuffing inmate property into a small locker.

Selena and the other officer glanced at each other when the lights flickered.

"Might get bad," he commented.

"Yeah."

"Do you need some help?"

Selena shook her head at the guard. "No, just wanted to talk with one of the inmates that was brought down earlier. Sam's coming in, too."

"Got your radio? If the lights keep flickering, the wing might lock down. You can radio out."

This would be the last place she'd want to be locked in. But with one touch of the radio, someone would unlock the door and let her out. The storm was giving her the heebie-jeebies.

As she was making her way to Rollos' cell, a lightning crack caused the lights to go off. Exactly what she didn't want to happen. Maybe the emergency generators would kick on quickly. Standing still, with her heart racing, she elected to await instructions from the bubble.

"Maldanado? 10-20? Did you just go in without me?" her radio crackled.

"Sam? Five feet inside A wing's door."

"Why didn't you wait? I specifically said to WAIT. I'll send someone out with a key." Sam's voice sputtered.

"10-4." Shouldn't be much more than a few seconds.

As Selena stood waiting by the property lockers, another thunderclap crashed on the roof above her. All of the inmates quieted.

Standing in the dark, Selena heard a sound she couldn't mistake. Pop. Pop. Pop. In rhythm, Selena listened as each of the segregated inmates' cell doors popped open. Instinctively, she moved back against a wall. Knowing there was nowhere in the wing to hide for security precautions, she also knew under the second floor and towards the corner was a spot that couldn't be seen by all the inmates unless they were outside their cell. Which she hoped didn't happen.

Silently, she slid her radio out of its holster and down to her side. Selena silenced her radio and tried to breathe. If any one of the inmates stepped out of their cell, she was history.

Selena closed her mouth and tried to even her breathing. The guards knew the doors were all unlocked now. Or did they? If power was out, would the board display open doors? The red lights might not come on, but surely, they'd see the doors opening.

Selena slowly raised her radio, so she could see her own little red dot glowing in the darkness. Her radio still worked, which was a good thing. As her eyes adjusted to the dimness, she saw doors slowly creep open around her. The inmates had figured out the popping noise. They were coming out.

Selena slid further down the wall. If the E-squad didn't come soon, the inmates were sure to see her shape flattened against the wall. They'd know exactly who she was if they came near because she intended to make as huge a racket as possible until someone saved her.

The inmates at opposite ends of the wing were beginning to mill around the locked area, shouting curses at one another, their vulgar language bouncing off the walls.

Dear Jesus. This situation was more than she could handle. She felt the darkness creeping in her vision for the second time that day. Fear settled in her chest as sweat dripped off her forehead. Be calm, be calm. Sam would come for her. Great time for God to jump in, too.

Selena tensed as the door closest to her quietly opened a crack. She felt the eyes peering out at her. She was dead. It wouldn't be a quiet death nor a painless one.

"Maldanado." The voice from the cell whispered.

Did she answer the voice? It sounded familiar

and yet, everyone in Administrative Segregation had spoken to her at some point.

"Maldanado." the voice whispered again, soft enough to be undetected by the growing buzz around her. "Hey, if you stay out there, they're going to kill you."

Well, he was right about that. Hopefully, they would kill her before they thought of anything else to do with her. A trapped corrections employee against many inmates she'd put in the Hole? She wouldn't live through it.

"Look, slide in here and shut the door. I promise I'll stay at the back of the cell."

Selena realized who the voice belonged to. Sam's clerk. She'd come out here to speak with him, actually interrogate him, and now she may have to rely on him.

"Are you crazy?" Selena broke her silence. His words dumbfounded her even if they sounded sincere and had a ring of hope in them.

"No, I'm not. I promise you'll be safe in here."

Sweet Jesus, please help. She called on the God she didn't know for help as if he knew who she was. She was desperate. That seemed like the only option. Except for crawling into the inmate's room who believed in that God. He had protected her once before, but this time wasn't a perceived threat. This was real, more real than she wanted to imagine.

"As soon as their eyes adjust, they'll see you. Please. I'll move to the back now."

Risking everything, she cautiously poked her head around the cracked door. The bed and sink and toilet were all where they should be with a huddled shape at the far end of the bed.

He was right. If they found her, she wouldn't survive against so many. But if she slid in and shut the door, it would be her against him. She might have a chance to save herself. The inmates loose in the wing wouldn't dare open a closed door, it was against unspoken inmate protocol. She could do this. Maybe? Selena wiped tears from her face. She had no choice.

She crawled in and pulled the door shut behind her. She curled up in a defensive ball to the left of the sink. As she watched the shadow on the bed, she quietly radioed her new location and an S.O.S. Selena pulled out her office keys with the other hand and prepared to fight for her life. Clawing his eyes out with a key would be tough.

Selena wiped sweat off her forehead; her eyes locked on the figure on the bed. She could confront him now while they were trapped in here. But she was on his territory; she had no leverage or desk to hide behind or guards around. If she incited him, his offer to stay where he was might change.

Selena laid her head back against the cool concrete wall. Her migraine was causing flashes of light in her eyes and a sick, knotted feeling in her bowels. If she didn't throw up in this cell, she was likely to once it was over. If it was ever going to be over.

The inmates outside the cell continued to ransack the housing unit wing, overturning tables and lockers, yelling curse words at each other. A pounding on the door caused her to jump and she pulled farther under the sink.

The shape on the bed moved silently toward her. Her eyes adjusted enough to see his face and his finger covering his lips.

Selena pressed herself farther into the hard wall as he came closer and closer. She was nearly under the sink by the time he crept past her to the door. She could smell the musky sweat on him, or was it her sweat? Please, please, please.

"Dude. Come on out." A loud voice from the other side of the door followed the pounding.

"NO. Not interested." Brandon called out.

"Okay, dude, you're missing the fun, though."

Selena could hear the other inmate move away from the door, taunting the officers. Brandon paused next to her. She gripped the keys tighter, ready to fight.

"Hey, it's going to be okay." Brandon reached out and patted her leg before returning to his spot on the bed; his features once again hidden. Selena nearly passed out.

~

Why had he touched her? Why had she let him? Brandon eased onto the bed and listened as the other inmates continued their rants and destruction. He had been frantic when the lights went off, and he realized Maldanado was still in the wing. And then when the doors popped open, shoot, he waited for her screams. She would have screamed, too, if any of the other Ad-Seg inmates had realized she was trapped in here with them.

Thank you, God. It was God who allowed her to be next to his door and within whispering distance when he'd taken a look outside his temporary confinement. Despite what he believed Maldanado may be involved with, he would have done anything to keep her safe. His thoughts were battered and torn. He was an inmate to her. She knew nothing about his undercover status. No one did. What she must think about his having her picture hidden in his cell. It was a con man type of thing to do.

And then he'd patted her and said it was going to be okay? He was crazy. Brandon could feel the fear dripping off her. Should he reveal who he really was? Maybe that was the thing to do. Praying silently, his heart wanted to, but the nudging he felt said to wait.

Watching from his corner, he could see her long legs folded up against herself and the radio and keys locked in clenched fists against her knees. In a different world, she would fit nicely….

What? What was he thinking with her paralyzed against his cell wall, expecting the door to be busted in at any moment? He was so stupid. And yet, she'd allowed him to momentarily comfort her instead of taking his hand off in pure panic. Could she sense his motive was pure and not evil? Brandon shook his head. For a moment, he had actually entertained ideas of Maldanado outside of this forsaken place.

"Why did you take my picture?" She whispered from her crouched position.

"What about you? The pot was…what? Not in my bunk. It isn't Watson's drug of choice, why was the pot there? You have to ask yourself that."

"I don't have to ask myself anything. You're the one who needs to answer the question." Selena pointed a finger at him, her voice low and threatening.

"Ah. With that attitude? You forget where you are. In my cell. Away from those out there." Brandon hated playing the nasty card, the one that put him in the same category as all of the other conning inmates. He had forced her to choose. Either him and the damage he could do to her reputation or the inmates running around in the wing, bent on destruction.

"That's pretty low."

"Why did you expect anything different?" She'd expected him to be different?

"I don't know. Sometimes you seem different, like you don't really belong here. Sam always talked highly of you. Up until now, you were respectful to me. And I believed it. Guess we were wrong."

Her words hurt. They weren't wrong, he was just playing a part. He couldn't tell her, at least not until he knew where she stood.

"Why did you take the picture?" Selena turned to him.

"Did you really find pot in the room?" Brandon countered.

"I… yes."

"Maldanado? Ma'am? I think you're in deep, up to your knees. Problem is, you're dealing with some really evil people. You are in trouble, bad trouble."

"How dare you." came her strangled reply.

Her response solidified what he had already suspected, she was in trouble.

Emergency lights sprang up in each of the rooms as the two heard whistles and shouts. "E-Squad. Everyone surrender to your rooms. Gas coming in."

Brandon sat up farther in the bed and caught

Selena's eye. She was about to be busted loose, but he knew his words had struck home. His statements brought truth to light, and he knew she truly was in trouble. He knew, she knew it, and whoever was in on the game knew it, too.

Small explosions sounded outside the room. Brandon tossed her his pillow and pulled a thin blanket up over his nose and mouth. They would be tasting and feeling the horrible sting of pepper spray soon as the e-squad took control of the wing. Selena, tears already coursing down her face, accepted the institutional pillow and covered her face as well.

35

Selena peeked through the glass window and came eye-to-eye with a black-suited guard.

"Maldanado. You okay?" He shouted around his gas mask.

She nodded and stumbled out the door. Glancing over her shoulder at Brandon, she noted he hadn't moved.

"Selena! Are you alright?" Sam caught her elbows as she wiped tears with the back of her hand.

"Was until you gassed the place." She coughed into the pillow.

"We didn't think we could get you out unless we did. The whole place erupted and with the lights out...well, what happened? You were supposed to wait for me. The Lieutenant said he found you in Rollos' cell? How did that happen?"

"Can you get me a glass of water first?" Selena glared at him through red-streaked eyes.

"Yes. Sorry. I was just worried and then when you came out and you were alright...." Sam filled a cup with water from the sink. She succumbed to the ministrations of a prison nurse who flushed her eyes of the vile gas.

"Okay, okay." Selena brushed the nurse away. "Yes, I went out to talk with Rollos without you and then the lights went out, cell doors popped open, and I was trapped."

"Yeah, I know."

"Well, Rollos offered the safety of his room."

"The safety of his…. Of all the…and you went?"

"What was I supposed to do? Wait for you to come get me? Nicely ask one of the inmates to please not hurt me?"

"No. But Rollos? Did he talk to you?"

"No, he just sat on the bed, and I stayed by the door waiting for someone to come get me."

"What a mess," Sam sat at his desk. "Do you need anything else? Because we're going to be here awhile writing reports."

"Maybe a Coke? And some aspirin?" Selena slumped into the chair across from him, her head threatening to spill wide open. A baseball bat to the brain might help.

Selena put her head down on her arms. She wished she could stay here for the next couple of hours, or maybe forever. Selena tossed the pillow onto the concrete at her feet. It smelled; something she hadn't noticed sitting confined to an inmate's cell while gas drifted under the door.

Sam brought what she'd asked for. Taking a gulp of Coke to swallow the pills, she eyed him. Furrows in his forehead, hair dripping wet, and a frown on his face, Sam looked ready to blow up.

"I'm sorry." Selena offered, wiping sweat from the sides of her face with the tail of her shirt.

"For what?" Sam asked. "For going in without me? For getting caught in a wing without electricity? For the doors popping open? For hanging out in an inmate's cell? No, not just any inmate, but THE inmate that took a personal item of yours?"

"Hanging out? Are you serious?" Selena lifted her head. He had lost his mind. All this and Sam had finally lost it.

"That's what I'm looking for, a little fire. You'd better get your senses about you, more than the last couple of weeks, because this thing is going to blow sky high when DeNickey gets back. If you thought his harassment was bad before, he's going to be looking for a cremation now." Sam said, standing with his back to her at the door.

"Somehow this is my fault?"

"No." Sam said softly, coming over to her side of the desk. "It's my fault, but, Selena, you haven't been yourself for a while now. You've been edgy, snippy, ready to strangle anyone who said 'Hi'. I don't know what's going on with you outside this place, but I'd bet my last dollar whatever it is, is bad. You're not eating, and I doubt you're sleeping."

Selena allowed herself a small hiccup. Sam, as always, was teaching, guiding, being her confidant, like he'd always been. He would help if he could, but she may be in over both their heads. She slumped farther in the seat.

"Hey," Sam continued. "If you want to tell me what's going on, do it now. This whole fiasco is going to get worse when DeNickey gets here, and somehow, he will make it out to be your fault. I don't plan to tell him about the stuff Rollos had in his cell, but it could get out. You have to be ready for this. I need you to be ready for this. Write your report from the time the lights went out, and we'll go over the rest when you're done."

"Okay." Selena finished the Coke. Sam left to meet with the officers and start their own reports of the incident. She knew he'd speak directly to the lieutenant who found her, and they'd compare notes. Again, she was in Sam's capable hands. Now if she could only deal with Jeremy the same way.

~

"Sir, we have a problem." The beefy sergeant of the housing unit approached Sam.

"What is it?" Sam blinked.

"One of the lockdown inmates is screaming for you."

"Aren't they all? Tell him to file a grievance."

"Sir, he's threatening to flood his cell and pitch a fit until you see him."

Sam knew what flooding the cell would look like. It would take another day just to clean up the mess.

"Fine, give me your pepper spray. He may not like my response. What cell number?"

"103, sir. You want some help?"

"Nope. I'm about to the breaking point, and I'd rather not have witnesses." Sam put the spray in his pants pocket and strode from the control area. He may have to go out with the guys tonight; he was definitely too wound to go home. Or maybe to the shooting range. He felt the need to hurt something.

Sam could hear the inmate pounding on his door, screaming every five seconds. He could see the other now contained inmates standing at their doorway with only the whites of their eyes showing.

As he walked up to the cell, he realized it was Rollos who was causing the disturbance. Anger welled up inside, threatening. He swallowed the urge to curse. He had been so wrong about his clerk. This crazy-acting man was nowhere close to the person Sam had started getting to know.

"Rollos, what do you want?"

Immediately, the pounding stopped.

"Come up closer to the door." Rollos whispered through the slit between the frame and the wall. "I really need to talk to you. Privately."

"Like that's going to happen. You've kind of blown that. I'm guessing the only time you were left alone in her office long enough to take the picture was when I left you in there, right?"

"Yes. But I need to tell you why. And it's about Maldanado."

"Talk. I'm listening." Sam leaned against the door jam. Whatever the inmate said was sure to be filled with lies.

"She's in trouble."

Sam closed his eyes again. He figured as much. Something was going on. The inmate wasn't threatening her; it was a simple statement of observation.

"With you? Seems like you're the one who had her stuff. If anyone was in deep, it would be you."

"No, not with me. I did take the stuff, but you have to believe me, it was for a good reason."

Sam snorted. He was a little surprised the inmate had actually confessed to stealing things. Rollos had to know he'd opened a can of worms with that confession.

"Seriously, she's really in trouble. Look, I've got outside contacts."

Who didn't?

"She's got to get out now before it goes any further. Tell her to take a leave of absence. Anything. Just get her out. If you care about her at all…"

Leave of absence? He'd never heard an inmate suggest that about a state employee. Usually, the statement was "I'll sue you" or "I'm going to make sure you're six feet under before I am", but never a leave of absence. What kind of game was he playing?

"Sam?"

Did he call him by his first name? Sam stood, baffled. None of this was making sense.

"What, Brandon?" Two could play that game.

"She's got to get out now. Jeremy…"

At the mention of Selena's boyfriend and the familiarity he'd used with both Sam and Jeremy's names, Sam turned and bolted for the back office.

36

Sam burst into his office. "That was Rollos, threatening to flood his cell. All because of you. Talking nonsense about you specifically. How you needed to get out, take a leave of absence, you're in too deep. Talking about Jeremy. Nothing he said made any sense. So, if you're going to talk and you want my help, now would be the perfect time." Sam jammed his fingers through his hair, causing it to spike up.

"Sam, I don't know."

"Selena, come on. We don't get to this point and wonder what just happened. There's got to be something. Think."

Sam didn't believe her. Didn't believe there was nothing between her and his clerk. His tone was terse, almost frightening. He'd never spoken to her that way before.

The phone rang before she could think of anything to say.

"Matthews. Yes sir. I'll send her right up." Sam dropped the phone back into its cradle. "And now, the warden wants to see you. Fantastic."

~

Selena sat in the Assistant Warden's office. The uncomfortable chair added to her growing alarm as she waited. Her first instinct had been to run out the front gates and never look back. Her second led her to his office. Did Jeremy know what was happening? She told him she was moving the stuff. But it was too soon for the authorities to know what had happened.

Everything would come out now. Surely, they'd find the missing pot from the confiscation room, tie it to her somehow, and she'd be fired. The pieces were about to fall.

The Assistant Warden was currently running the prison while the Warden himself was out at the conference with DeNickey. A thin, black man with years of experience in state and federal institutions, he had an easy laugh and a laid-back personality. She also saw him as a person who was fair, a thinker, and usually an ally. His long pauses between his thoughts and words were intimidating at the very least, but Selena had come to expect them.

"Do you know why you're here? In my office?" Mr. Warren asked.

Selena refused to visually quake although everything in her wanted to.

"No, sir." A different setting would have allowed her to call him by his first name, Rick, but saying his given name now was out of line.

"We have us a situation." Mr. Warren drew out his words.

"Yes, sir."

"It seems as if Mr. DeNickey was picked up today by the DEA." Mr. Warren let his words settle over her.

"He what?" Selena startled in her chair. The pain killers had helped for a time with the migraine, but she felt its return like a locomotive. "What does that mean, sir?"

"Just what I said. Apparently, he was involved in some shady stuff outside the prison. They caught up with him at the conference." Mr. Warren leaned toward her, hands templed on the desk. "And there's evidence your FBI boyfriend was involved, too. However, he can't be found at this moment."

Selena noticed through the glass door guards were posted outside Mr. Warren's office. Would they come in now, put the cuffs on her? Selena looked at the nearby trash can. She'd be able to reach it in time if the bile in her throat ever made it farther. She tried to breathe deep, but she was quickly using up all the oxygen in the room.

"Um…I don't really know what to say."

"What I gather from Sam is you've not been yourself lately, and he thinks more is going on than you can handle."

Traitor.

"The common denominator, as I'm sure you've realized, is you. DeNickey's team of investigators, FBI boy's girlfriend…you're it. You're the commonality."

"But…but I didn't know…" Selena hated the trap she found herself in.

"You didn't know DeNickey had a drug connection with someone outside the prison, and your boyfriend just may be that 'someone'?"

Silence.

"Did they ever ask you to do anything illegal,

inside or outside the prison?" Mr. Warren leaned back in his chair. "No, stop. Don't answer that. No one's read you your rights."

"My rights, sir? Am I being arrested?"

The phone rang and Mr. Warren stared at her for a long moment.

"Warren's office." Listening intently when he picked the receiver up, he doodled on his notepad. "And you believe this? You've checked it out? A'right."

"Selena." Mr. Warren hung up and turned his attention to her. "Selena, I have always liked you. You're a strong employee, a female to be reckoned with, a little on the green side, but you're a fast learner and loyal. You already know how Sam feels about you, and I trust Sam."

Any minute and the guards would come in and take her to lock-up.

"I believe you have been misused by some very bad people and they've asked you to do things that are totally against your ethics. They fed on that, tripped you, and left you to land in the situation you're in right now. Luckily, there were other people monitoring the situation; albeit disappointed in your involvement that can vouch for your intent and are recommending you be released from your post without arrest."

Without arrest. Released from her post. He didn't know she'd planted the pot. Mr. Warren didn't know.

"Gather up your stuff. You'll be walked out and off the grounds immediately."

Off the grounds. But not arrested?

Shaking, Selena stood when Mr. Warren did. Giving instructions to the guard, he allowed her to leave. Selena walked heavily to her office with her escort close behind.

"Ma'am?" the guard Mr. Warren had chosen for her spoke.

"Yes?" Selena struggled through tears. If she didn't make eye contact with anyone, she could make it through this humiliation. She hoped Sam didn't try to reach her. She couldn't bear to look at him right now.

"I don't know what this is all about, but everyone likes you here. We always have. Seems like a wrong place, wrong time thing." The burly guard looked close to tears himself. "Anyway, like I said, I don't know what this is about, but if you need anything, you let me know."

"Thanks." Selena gave him a half-smile. "My advice to you is to keep your eyes open and your mouth shut."

"Yes, ma'am."

Selena swiped the remaining pictures from her desk, a forgotten toothbrush from the drawer, and personal odds and ends around the office.

Walking out with her escort, she was thankful Sam stayed away. He was surely embarrassed, disheartened, disillusioned. Mr. Warren met her at the front doors and although he was doing his duty, it obviously saddened him as well. Selena left, tears streaming down her face.

~

Sam slammed the phone down. He'd tried calling Selena's cell phone multiple times and left multiple messages. Picking it back up, he dialed the administration building.

"The assistant warden, please." Sam waited. "Rick, what happened? Word is she was escorted out?"

"You know I don't have to tell you any of this."

"I know, I know. But this is Selena. Please. What'd she do? And DeNickey?"

"Word travels fast. DEA picked him up at the conference, put him in handcuffs in front of everyone."

"That's been a long time coming, sir."

"I know. Selena was fired without charges. I can't say any more than that except it seems like an inside informant spoke up on her behalf. Know anything about that?" Rick went on before Sam could respond. "And this FBI boyfriend? He's in the wind."

Sam frowned. Inside informant. Brandon? He'd been frantic until Sam had finally gone out to his cell. Brandon had begged him to talk with Selena and warn her. Almost protective of her.

"I don't know anything about Jeremy, except he's a scumbag."

"Well, if you do hear anything, don't call me. I've got my hands full with this internal investigation. At least until the warden gets back."

After Selena had gotten called up to the administration building, E-squad had come back down and pulled Brandon from his cell. Whatever was happening was happening fast. Sam was aware of the need to move troublesome inmates out of an institution quickly, especially if they had been caught involved with a staff member, but this? There were so many moving parts. Sam wanted time to investigate, and the administration had pulled all of the players off the field.

Sam pulled out his copy of Brandon's visitor log. He was sorry to see him go, but how was he involved with Selena?

Something pulled at him. Something about what he'd said and how familiar he'd been with both Selena and Sam and Jeremy's first names. As Sam was taking Brandon's file up for the transfer, he'd flipped through it and hadn't found anything out of place. Still…

There was only one name on the visitor log. Apparently, Brandon didn't have family around, or ones that acknowledged him. Only the girl on the sheet had visited and not as regularly as a girlfriend might. Suzie Winters. Sam opened his computer and typed in her name. Maybe something would click if he looked her up. He fully expected a Facebook account or a "Did you go to school with…?' to pop up. Instead, he got an article in the Los Angeles Times. The woman in the picture was a slim, long-haired blonde. This couldn't be her. The caption read Officer Winters Receives Award. Sam snatched the phone and called the visiting room extension.

"Visiting room. Sgt. Walters."

"Sergeant, this is Sam in Lockdown. Do you normally work third shift?"

"Yeah, unfortunately. Most trouble comes knocking at my door."

"Do you happen to remember a visitor who came to see my clerk, Rollos?"

"Ha. Do I? I always thought how does Sam get

the best gigs, all the way down to the good-looking visitors of his clerk?"

"You want to trade?"

"Nope, too much paperwork for me."

"So, about Brandon's visitor." Sam reminded him.

"Oh yeah, leggy blonde. Cute."

"Anything strike you about her? Besides her looks?"

"Not really. They acted like brother and sister, though, not girlfriend/boyfriend stuff."

"Thanks, Sergeant." Sam set the phone down and looked at the article again.

But why would an officer visit an inmate in Oklahoma? Family? If they were, they were adopted. Brandon's dark olive skin contrasted greatly with Officer Winters pale complexion.

Sam read farther. Deeply buried in the article was another picture of the officer. A familiar face standing just behind her made his heart stop. The caption read "Officer Winters' partner, Brandon Sollor, was unavailable for comment."

Inmate Brandon Rollos in a U.S. Marshal's jacket.

37

"Sam?" Selena pulled the cell phone closer to her ear. Perched on the rocking chair in the front porch shadow, Selena frowned.

"Selena. Why haven't you returned my calls?" Sam's voice on the other end was hard to hear from the other prison sounds behind him.

"Look, I just wanted to say thanks for being there for me. You can't possibly know all that's happened."

"First you get called up front and then I hear DeNickey has been taken into custody by Drug Enforcement officers. And to top it all off, you were walked out under escort? What happened? Warren said you were released from your post, but it was without charges." Sam sounded frustrated.

Selena said a quick, silent blessing for Mr. Warren. He didn't have to spin it favorably.

"And then Brandon…" Sam started.

"Sam, stop. I'm not coming back but I wanted you to know that I'm good here. I'll talk to you another time. Bye." Selena felt the memories crowd her. One brutal memory after another assaulted her. Nothing about the prison had been easy. In fact, now separated from it, Selena looked back and realized it had been one of the darkest times of her life.

Selena pulled up to the ranch house and held the door open for Patches. Pausing for a moment, she banged her toes together and knocked the dust off. She'd forgotten how hard the work could be around the ranch. Mind-numbing, brainless work. She welcomed it. She still had yet to wake in the morning and not wonder why she was at the ranch, in her old bedroom, with the smell of clover wafting through the screened window.

The young investigator with big dreams thought she owned the world; in reality, it owned her, molding her into a person she didn't like and never wanted to be.

She found herself sobbing often by She'Daisy's stall with Patches whining at her feet, physically sick about how stupid she'd been. To let herself get caught like that in such a mess. And to think that she could handle it on her own. Selena's thoughts turned to the worn laundry she saw through the barn window, hanging on the line, washed out blue cloths flapping in the breeze. That's what she was, a wash-out.

Heaviness was her companion when she took She'Daisy out for a run. Thinking she could outrace the heartache, she'd urged the horse faster and faster until the wind whipped around her head and disguised the tears of grief.

She released She'Daisy to the side pasture and shook the dirt off the saddle blanket.

"Hey, pokey, Patches already beat you inside." Ben, coming out from the barn, slapped at her with his straw cowboy hat.

"I'm coming." Selena took her own hat off and brushed at her jeans.

"Race ya!" Ben started off in a lope, looking over his shoulder for her response.

When Selena didn't follow, Ben circled back around and stood just inches in front of her. Standing taller than her, he craned his neck down looking first at her boots and then up at her eyes. Selena watched him warily.

Ben picked up his foot and dropped it hard on hers.

"Ow. What'd you do that for?" She retorted, stepping back.

"Because I can." His reply brought him up in front of her again. Lifting his boot again, he dropped it on the other foot.

"Ben. That hurts." Selena punched him hard in the arm.

When he punched her back, she slapped him across the face. After a stunned look, Ben sideswiped her feet. Selena fell backwards and landed on the unforgiving ground.

"You!" Nostrils flaring, she scrambled up.

"It's 'bout time you started getting angry." Ben hollered. He was able to block her punches until his boots tripped over a boot-scraper in the yard. Locking his arms around her, they both fell in the dust. Ben scrambled to straddle her. Selena noted the trickle of blood from a busted lip and winced, knowing she'd caused the injury. Still spouting mad, she struggled against his control, trapped between his knees.

Selena saw blue sky as a strong hand lifted Ben off her and tossed him to the side. She scrambled up and came face-to-face with the inmate from the prison.

"Maldanado." He stepped toward her.

"How…? What are you…?" Selena glanced at Ben, still in the dirt.

Rollos. How did he get out? Did he escape? Why was he here?

"Just listen for a second." The inmate pulled out a badge. "I'm US Marshal. And its Sollor, Brandon Sollor. I was working undercover in the prison."

"You are WHAT?"

Ben stood up next to her. "Selena, do you know this guy?"

"I don't believe you. I don't know how you got out or how you found me or what you want. Ben, call the cops."

"Wait, I promise you, I'm a US Marshal. Just give me a minute."

"You promise me? Promise? I think you're a lying, evil man. Sorry, correction, inmate, not man."

"Selena. Okay, go ahead and call the cops. They'll confirm who I am. Please."

"So, what if I imagine, for a moment, that you are who you say you are. What do you want?"

"I thought, maybe, we could talk about what happened."

"Nothing happened. Nothing that needs to be explained. Or talked about. Ever." Selena motioned to Ben. "Don't call the cops for now. I think I can handle this."

"Like you did at the prison?" Brandon hesitated.

"Really? If you were really undercover, do you realize what you put me through? Did you not know what they were doing to me? Did you think with that little peon brain of yours how all of this could affect me and my family?" Selena attacked. "When you were playing hero in your cell, did you have a clue what you were doing?"

"You did put pot in my cell and set me up." Brandon tilted his head at her. "Selena, wait, I wasn't playing hero. I was genuinely concerned for your safety."

"YEAH, and you stole stuff from my office. And DeNickey and Jeremy, know about them? They threatened to send my father back across the border. After DeNickey's thugs beat up Jeremy. AND because I thought it was my way out." Selena outstretched her hands. "Let me see that again."

Brandon handed her his badge.

Selena looked it over, threw it in the dirt, and stomped on it. "I CANNOT believe this. Could you have stepped in any sooner?"

"I completed my mission, and DeNickey got locked up. And I do know about your FBI friend, but what I don't know is where he is. I vouched for you with the powers-that-be and explained how you were involved, which was very minor, and gave you a different fate than the two you were running with. And," he picked up his wallet and blew the dirt off, "I came out to check on you and see if Jeremy was with you."

"How nice of you." Selena spat. "Two very different things, checking on me and checking on me to see if Jeremy was with me. I haven't seen Jeremy since I left the prison. Go look somewhere else. Get away from me."

She walked to her Blazer and got in. Brandon opened the passenger door and sat on the seat next to her.

"Get out." Tears sprang to Selena's eyes. She pounded the steering wheel and started the engine.

"Listen, he may try to find you. He's into bigger things than you can imagine." Brandon backed out of the truck.

"He said he wanted to be closer to his sister, that's all I know." Selena sniffed. "He wouldn't come here. He wouldn't dare."

"Ok, well, he's my loose end. So please…" Brandon scratched his number on a slip of paper. "Where's his sister at? Do you know?"

"Dallas, I think." Selena wiped her nose.

"Look, can we just talk a little bit? Maybe go get coffee."

Selena turned off the truck. With a sullen frown and a loud sigh, she drug her feet to the wrap-around porch. Brandon followed quietly.

"Can I get you some lemonade?" Jolie bustled out, Papá and Ben standing just inside the screen door.

"No." Selena said.

"Yes, ma'am." Brandon countered.

Selena glared at him.

"Should I start explaining? Or do you have questions?"

"Are you just that dumb? Of course, I have questions. But I'd love to hear your story first."

Brandon grimaced. "Okay, I went undercover at

the prison several months ago because we ran across an outside dealer who was running his mouth about his cousin inside the prison. The inmate said he could get any drug he wanted through dirty guards."

"Go on."

"I went UC to help the Feds with their investigation. The investigator's office came up, which led me to you and DeNickey. My partner on the outside, she would do her job on the street and then report back to me as a visitor. Which is how Jeremy came into the picture. Through you."

Selena chewed her nails.

"Stop." Brandon cautiously placed his hand over hers, stopping the nail biting.

"I trusted you because Sam trusted you." Selena pulled her hand away.

"There's no way you could have known this, but once I realized you were being victimized, you could have trusted me regardless of Sam. That's why I convinced you to come into my cell during the riot. That's the safest place you could have been on the whole property. And the time with the fight on the yard? Remember, I told you to get inside?"

Selena did remember and other times when the inmate – scratch that – Marshal – Ugh – Brandon had been respectful. She'd never thought about him in any other light other than a kind inmate. If she were honest, she'd been slightly attracted to that kindness. Selena shook her head. Dios mio, what was she thinking?

"I cannot believe that I didn't know."

"No one did. Not even the warden. If I felt you or I were unsafe, I would have told my partner to pull the plug."

"What now?" Selena's pulse quickened as he turned toward her. Taking a deep breath, she tried not to look at him. Everything in her screamed "he's still an inmate." No, he's not. Funny how her view of him changed with his simple explanation. He had been a very good-looking inmate, but she never glanced twice due to her status as investigator and his, an inmate. Now, he was a very good-looking US Marshal.

"Well, if you'll allow it, I think I'll stick around for a bit and see if Jeremy shows up. I don't think he will, but he might."

Selena shrugged. Stick around for a bit? "I don't need protecting."

"I'm very aware of that. I'd just like to lock up Jeremy for his part in all this." Brandon stuck his hand out. "Shake on it? This new start?"

Selena questioned her wisdom in taking his hand. "It's going to take some getting used to, seeing you as law enforcement and not an inmate."

"I know. Look at me." Brandon brought her eyes to his. "I'm not an inmate, and I'm not Jeremy."

That would be the harder part. She knew now that he was undercover, but she had trusted Jeremy because he was FBI. Could she trust Brandon? He was law enforcement, too.

39

Selena stood on the top railing of the arena, watching Ben attempt to ride a green horse. The poor horse had bucked him off twice already, but Ben continued to wipe the grit from his eyes and grab the reins again.

She looked at the line of dust coming in from the west. Another Cowboy Action Shooting competition was about to be under way. She breathed in the summer air and counted her blessings.

"Hey, cowgirl." Brandon put his arm across her shoulders.

Selena grinned at him. He'd done just what he said he'd do and stuck around. Slowly, she'd allowed him into her world, a coffee date here and a ride around the ranch there. And just as slowly, started accepting his attention and warm hugs. Brandon had become one of those blessings she counted in her life. His calm attitude and gentle words undid parts of her heart she thought would be locked up forever. Betrayal was a hard knot to undo. She felt safe in his presence and thankful he was showing her he was who he said he was. His intentions towards her caused schoolgirl flutters and a depth of emotions a relationship with Jeremy could never reach. Trust was hard and not easily given, but every word Brandon spoke lined up with his actions. The integrity with which he lived his life and how he treated her spoke volumes towards the man she was coming to love.

"What'd you think about church yesterday?" She turned to him. "I'm curious. You said you weren't religious when you were in prison."

"I'm still not. Religion is different than a true Christ-follower. And especially nothing like what you saw in the prison." Brandon slid his hand into hers and drew her over to a bale of hay. Not releasing her hand, he gently smiled at her. "I think it's interesting the pastor talked about freedom, exactly what we talked about. And the scripture in Romans. I'm pretty sure God played a big part in this. In us."

"I thought that, too." Selena looked at their hands, still intertwined. "I think freedom looks different for many people. With you, I could never understand why you seemed so much freer than I was, and I wasn't locked up."

"You thought about me?" Brandon elbowed her.

"No, yes. Well, in some ways." Selena swatted at him.

"Think about me now?"

Selena shook her head and stood. Yes, she did. "Sometimes. Remind me about the verse in Romans?"

"The scripture said 'all things work together for good.' I think that's where we're at, the good." Brandon looked up, holding her with his gaze. "Do you feel freer now?"

"I do. I don't think I knew how heavy everything was weighing on me. It was like I was living out my dream, but it felt like dead weight. And honestly, somewhere I lost myself. Covering up who I truly was to impress others or fuel their expectations or even be who they wanted me to be. And before, I didn't think about God very much, didn't think he was interested in me. But I hear you talk about Him, and I think, maybe I was wrong. Maybe He is a little more involved than I thought, you know? "

"I know you impress me. Just by being you."

"Hopefully I am me now." Selena squinted her eyes. "So, do you think about me?"

"Nope. Just every other second." Brandon caught her hands again. "What's a guy gotta do to kiss a pretty cowgirl?"

"Nothing. Just be you." Selena pressed her lips to his.

EPILOGUE

Jeremy pulled his hat farther down on his head and watched Selena complete her competition run. With her long hair pulled high on her head and her hat flying behind, he remembered the times he had pulled on those curls.

It was dangerous and foolish for him to be here. He'd gotten as far away as possible when he heard DeNickey was picked up.

The boots he'd pulled out of the closet for the trip rubbed his ankles. Dust settled on the toes. In fact, dust covered every inch of his being from the straw cowboy hat to his alligator skin boots.

He clenched his hands at his side and forced out a breath. She couldn't see him. Growing the beard and letting his hair fall in shaggy lengths might not have been such a great idea. It made him look wild and a little crazy, but purposefully covered most of his face.

He'd caused so much damage.

He moved out beyond the railing, back towards the shadowy parts of the makeshift town designed for the competition. Circling around the crowds mingling in faux doorways and tipping his hat to a group of ladies dressed in saloon wear, he slouched toward the other side of the arena. His gaze swept over the people. One more glimpse and he'd disappear.

~

Brandon swung open the gate as She'Daisy skidded into the holding pen, dust flying.

"That was a pretty good run, don't you think?" Selena slid onto the ground and untangled her curls from the hat strings. She threw her arms around him.

"I do. Maybe you'll beat Ben this time." Brandon smiled at her excitement and kissed her nose. "You did good, cowgirl."

Looking over her shoulder, Brandon caught eyes with a man standing across the pen. Jeremy.

"Selena, go. Jeremy's here. Find Ben and stay with him." Brandon pushed her away and ran around the cattle chutes to where he'd last seen Jeremy. He couldn't have gone far. He knew Jeremy would come back, confirming his fears that Jeremy hadn't ditched Selena yet.

Over by the boardwalk, a man strode, zigzagging through the crowd that had come to watch the competition. Brandon broke into a run and dodged behind the buildings. Racing to the parking area, he followed Jeremy to a non-descript sedan. He reached out and caught the door. Jeremy swung at him. Dodging the left-handed hook, Brandon grabbed Jeremy's shirt and threw him to the ground. Wrestling him in the dirt, Brandon punched him in the gut. The sound of one of Jeremy's ribs popped with the thud. Brandon flipped Jeremy on his belly and put handcuffs around his wrists. Jeremy lay heaving great breathes of air.

"It's over, Jeremy." Brandon stood. The sound of sirens filled the air.

"Are you okay?" Selena rushed at him, Ben close behind her. Selena glanced at Jeremy as a cop put him in the back seat of the squad car.

"Yes. I knew he'd come back." Brandon succumbed to her touch as she ran cool fingertips over his face, arms, chest, looking for damage. "I'm really okay. Who called the cops?"

"Ben did after I told him what was going on. We followed the sirens."

"Come here." Brandon wrapped his arms around Selena, his hands wide on her back. The cop car rolled by and gave them a stiff wave. Jeremy refused to look at them. "I'm fine. This is over finally. We don't have to wonder if he'll step back in our lives. I'm definitely looking forward to a new start."

"Me, too."

"I'll always protect you. Always."

"I know."

Ben cheered as Brandon kissed her.

"Remember that verse we talked about in Romans? 'All things work for good'? I think that is truly where we are now."

"And free."

"Yes, and free."

Julie Brown writes from her back porch in Missouri where the hummingbirds fly, the coffee is sweet, and friends are welcomed. She has a degree in Criminal Justice and has worked with juvenile offenders, teens in crisis, and in a prison facility. Julie has published an inspirational book titled "EVEN WHEN: God's promises are still true" about her journey through grief and loss.

Social Media

Facebook: *https://www.facebook.com/julie.brown.5015983*

Website: *working on it*

Pinterest: *https://www.pinterest.com/jewels05/*

Blog: https://juleskeepsakebox.wordpress.com/ *(I clearly have not kept up on this, but I want to resurrect it ☺)*

List of all published books

EVEN WHEN: God's promises are still true